Everything was the same, yet everything was different.

Caught in a pool of light at the back of a downtown shopping mall, Batman and Robin were surrounded by weapon-wielding thugs they'd caught red-handed in a late-night heist. Three thugs were already down on the ground, in no condition to continue the fight; but another four were armed and willing.

The Dynamic Duo worked well together, covering each other's back, one ducking to allow the other to get in a cross-blow at their attackers. That's how it was the same.

The difference was, the man in the cape and cowl wasn't Bruce Wayne.

For thirty nights now, Jean Paul Valley had been the Batman. Night after night like some monstrous bird of prey, Batman swooped through Gotham City. His new costume, born of Jean Paul Valley's fevered trance, made him far more dangerous, more sinister, than ever before.

*Truly this is the role I have been born for,* he thought to himself. *I will be the best Batman there could ever be.*

# BATMAN®

# KNIGHTFALL
# & BEYOND

## Alan Grant

Interior pencil art by
## Graham Nolan

Interior inks by
## Scott Hanna

Batman created by Bob Kane

**BANTAM BOOKS**

New York • Toronto • London • Sydney • Auckland

RL 5.5, 008-012
BATMAN: KNIGHTFALL & BEYOND
A Skylark Book/August 1994

Skylark Books is a registered trademark of Bantam Books,
a division of Bantam Doubleday Dell Publishing Group, Inc.
Registered in U.S. Patent and Trademark Office and elsewhere.

Cover painting by Joe DeVito.
Interior pencil art by Graham Nolan.
Interior inks by Scott Hanna.

Batman created by Bob Kane.

The stories, characters, and incidents featured in this publication
are entirely fictional.

ISBN 0-553-48187-8

*Published simultaneously in the United States and Canada*

*Bantam Books are published by Bantam Books, a division of Bantam Double-
day Dell Publishing Group, Inc. Its trademark, consisting of the words
"Bantam Books", and the portrayal of a rooster, is Registered in U.S. Patent
and Trademark Office and in other countries. Marca Registrada. Bantam
Books, 1540 Broadway, New York, New York 10036.*

PRINTED IN THE UNITED STATES OF AMERICA

OPM   0   9   8   7   6   5   4   3   2   1

To my parents, Ron and Renc,
who understood that a boy needs his comics.

# Acknowledgments

With respectful thanks to Bob Kane, who created a legend; to Bill Finger, writer; and to the Bat-crew, Denny, Doug, Chuck, Scott, Jordan, and Darren, who did all the hard work.

*Batman: Knightfall & Beyond* was primarily adapted from the story serialized in the following comic books, originally published by DC Comics:

*Batman* #488-510 (1993–94)
*Batman: Shadow of the Bat* #16-30 (1993–94)
*Detective Comics* #656-677 (1993–94)
*Legends of the Dark Knight* #59-63 (1993–94)
*Robin* #1, 7-9 (1993–94)

These comic books were created by the following people:

| | | | |
|---|---|---|---|
| Editors: | Dennis O'Neil | Inkers: | Jim Aparo |
| | Scott Peterson | | Terry Austin |
| | Archie Goodwin | | Eduardo Barreto |
| | | | John Beatty |
| Assistant | | | Bret Blevins |
| Editors: | Jordan B. Gorfinkel | | Norm Breyfogle |
| | Darren Vincenzo | | Rick Burchett |
| | Jim Spivey | | Steve George |
| | Christopher Duffy | | Vince Giarrano |
| | | | Dick Giordano |
| Writers: | Chuck Dixon | | Scott Hanna |
| | Alan Grant | | Ray Kryssing |
| | Doug Moench | | Tom Mandrake |
| | Dennis O'Neil | | Mike Manley |
| | | | Ron McCain |
| Pencillers: | Jim Aparo | | Luke McDonnell |
| | Jim Balent | | Frank McLaughlin |
| | Eduardo Barreto | | Josef Rubinstein |
| | Bret Blevins | | Bob Smith |
| | Norm Breyfogle | | Bob Wiacek |
| | Vince Giarrano | | |
| | Tom Grummett | Colorists: | Adrienne Roy |
| | Barry Kitson | | Digital Chameleon |
| | Tom Mandrake | | |
| | Mike Manley | Letterers: | Jim Aparo |
| | Michael Netzer | | Ken Bruzenak |
| | Graham Nolan | | John Costanza |
| | Ron Wagner | | Albert DeGuzman |
| | | | Tim Harkins |
| | | | Todd Klein |
| | | | Willie Schubert |
| | | | Richard Starkings |

With additional material adapted from:

*Batman: Venom* (1993)
(Originally published as *Legends of the Dark Knight* #16-20, 1991)

| | | | |
|---|---|---|---|
| Editors: | Andrew Helfer | Inker: | José Luis Gracía-López |
| | Kevin Dooley | Colorist: | Steve Oliff |
| Writer: | Dennis O'Neil | Letterer: | Willie Schubert |
| Layouts: | Trevor Von Eeden | | |
| Penciller: | Russell Braun | | |

*Batman: Sword of Azarel* (1993)
(Originally published as *Batman: Sword of Azrael* #1-4, 1992)

| | | | |
|---|---|---|---|
| Editor: | Archie Goodwin | Inker: | Kevin Nowlan |
| Assistant | | Colorist: | Lovern Kindzierski |
| Editor: | Bill Kaplan | Letterer: | Ken Bruzenak |
| Writer: | Dennis O'Neil | | |
| Penciller: | Joe Quesada | | |

*Batman: Vengeance of Bane* Special #1 (1993)

| | | | |
|---|---|---|---|
| Editor: | Dennis O'Neil | Inker: | Eduardo Barreto |
| Assistant | | Colorist: | Adrienne Roy |
| Editor: | Scott Peterson | Letterer | Bill Oakley |
| Writer: | Chuck Dixon | | |
| Penciller: | Graham Nolan | | |

**BATMAN**

**BRUCE WAYNE**

**ROBIN**

**THE NEW BATMAN**

**AZRAEL**

**JEAN PAUL VALLEY**

**BANE**

**BIRD**

**TROGG**

**LADY SHIVA**

**MAD HATTER**

**KILLER CROC**

**TIM DRAKE**

**ALFRED PENNYWORTH**

**COMMISSIONER JAMES GORDON**

**JACK DRAKE**

**DR. SHONDRA KINSOLVING**

**BENEDICT ASP**

**ZOMBIE**

**SIR HEMINGFORD GRAY**

**NIGHTWING**

**POISON IVY**

**SCARECROW**

**ABATTOIR**

# Prologue

**N**ight falls on Gotham City. The shadows that have been lengthening for the past hour suddenly take a last leap, and daylight is banished.

The lights have long since twinkled on, whole buildings bursting into checkerboard life. Now the streets are alive with piercing headlamps and impatient engines. The exodus has begun. The citizens are anxious to be home, safe and warm, out of the chill city wind that the high towers funnel into never-ending gusts—away from the fears and nameless dread that nighttime brings.

A big yellow moon is rising, its face scuffed by a dirty cloud. A noticeable thrill runs through the ugly, litter-strewn streets. In the shadows there's a stirring. Criminal eyes gleam dully. The night people are making ready.

They say Gotham was designed by a madman: thrusting Gothic spires like jungle trees compete for the light; elevated railway tracks stalk between them like some giant, mutant insect. But there's one place from which even Gotham City looks beautiful.

Perched on a grotesque stone gargoyle a hundred stories above street level, the black-garbed crusader called the Batman tastes the night. His eyes narrow behind his mask, and his cape whips behind him in the breeze.

At ground level the city is dirty, run-down, and dangerous, but from up here Gotham looks like an entirely different place. It stretches before him, a panorama of light, a glittering fantasyland that completely contradicts its ugly reality.

B–A–T—His peripheral vision picks up the neon letters, flashing intensely. He recognizes the giant billboard in Gotham Square, two blocks away and a hundred feet lower. BATH-TIME SHOULD BE FUN-TIME!

Beneath him, spotlights blaze on lower rooftops, intense beams cleaving the air in computer-controlled patterns; meant as decoration, they suddenly remind him of a city at war.

And so it is—a war against crime.

Far below, his keen eyes pick out a small group—a man, woman, and a boy. A family, going to the movies. For an instant his mind flashes back to that awful night, more than twenty years before. He had a family then. His father was a doctor and more often than not worked nights. It was a special treat when they all went out together.

Shards of memory once again reel past his mind's eye—how excited he was the night they saw *The Mark of Zorro*. Leaving the cinema, his heart and head full. Then the sudden, confused change—dark shadows where before there was light. A slimy-looking man with dead fish eyes and a gun. A whiny voice demanding, "Gimme the jewels!"

He remembers his mother's fear—his father's defiant courage—while he stood by openmouthed. The gun roared—once, twice—filling his head with thunder. Then running footsteps, and a terrible, deathly silence as he stared at the bodies on the ground and the ever-widening pool of blood.

He remembers the sick despair, the terrible loss, the lonely grief. The funeral and after, just a little boy standing on the windswept grave with tears on his cheeks and his clenched fists defying the storm.

He remembers the oath he swore—that as he grew to manhood he would do everything in his power to prevent evil from ever befalling another innocent soul.

Now, two decades later—twenty years of extensive training and in-depth education—the orphan stands high on a gargoyle atop of Wayne Tower. He is what he has made himself—the protector and defender of this city and its people. He is the Batman.

The wind gusts. Did he hear . . . ? Yes—a frightened plea, a muffled threat drifting up in the chill night air.

He stands to his full height. For a moment he is silhouetted against the moon, a symbol of justice and retribution.

Then he dives, and plunges down, down, down.

# PART I

# KNIGHTFALL

# One

**S**cream an' I'll trash ya, sucker!" Crazybob hissed.

Moonlight glinted on the tire iron he hefted, and Charles Lowton's heart sank even further. He took a frightened step back, but the bony fingers of Lou and Mook, Crazybob's thug companions, closed on his arms.

"Get his wallet 'n watch!" Hands fumbled at his jacket pocket, and Charles opened his mouth to yell.

"I warned ya!" Crazybob raised his hand. "I trash screamers!"

Charles watched, horrified, as the deadly metal began to arc down toward him. *Please! Let me wake up and find out it's a nightmare!*

Then something happened that Charles Lowton couldn't explain. Something came spinning out of the darkness and hit Crazybob's hand with an audible crunch. He yelped with pain as his weapon tumbled to the sidewalk.

Mook let out a startled gasp. Out of the corner of his eye, Charles saw something black and ragged edged outlined against the moon, swooping toward them like . . . some monstrous bat.

There was a muffled cry, followed by the sounds of men who've had the wind knocked out of them.

Twin gunshots suddenly boomed out. Crazybob had hauled a pistol from his belt and was brandishing it wildly, blasting into the darkness of the alley.

"Bad move." The voice sounded like gravel, or broken glass, and even as Crazybob looked up, that terrible moving darkness fell on him.

Batman had dropped 150 feet in freefall before his right hand stretched out. Long, hard years of practice had honed his abilities to a finesse approachable only by Olympic champions. At exactly the right moment, he tossed a Batarang, his Batline attached. It snaked through the air to loop with unerring accuracy around a flagpole protruding from the top of an office block. The muscles of his arm rippled under his tight, dark costume as it took the strain, swinging as the line went taut, his momentum carrying him forward.

He landed on a low, flat roof, his billowing cape steadying him, and the line retracted into its special holder. He caught the glint of a weapon below and sent a Batarang spinning from the supply he carried in his utility belt.

As was always his way, befitting the master of a dozen different martial arts, Batman had taken the thugs out with minimum violence. Normally he'd have given them a chance to surrender, but these three were only seconds away from committing murder. So he'd disabled them and left them for the police. It wasn't his role to judge or punish them; that was for the duly elected judicial process.

Charles Lowton didn't open his eyes until the flashing blue light and whooping sirens of the police car stopped beside him.

By then Batman was half a block away, his Batline soaring twenty yards up to clutch a heavy aerial. Another innocent saved . . . and yet the war against crime would never end.

The line jerked. He looked up, puzzled. Standing on the edge of the roof, one hand grasping the taut Batline, was a tall, muscular figure. His chest was like a barrel, his neck thick and powerful, and the red eyepieces in the hood that covered his head gave him a grim air of almost alien menace.

"My name is Bane!" the man thundered. "I'm going to destroy you piece by piece!"

The Batline jerked again as Bane grabbed it in both hands, wrapping it around his knuckles. He wore only a thin vest for protection, and his muscles bulged underneath.

*Impossible!* Batman thought. *That line has a breaking strain far in excess of anything any man can generate.*

"And then I'm going to break you like a twig!"

The line snapped, and Batman dropped. No time to throw another line—he had no choice but to rely on his athleticism. The billowing cape acted as a drag, slowing his plunge; ankles bent, he landed, rolling easily and lightly to his feet and facing upward.

Bane was gone.

Batman was used to threats from criminals—but Bane's incredible strength, and the conviction with which he'd uttered his words, marked him as someone truly dangerous. Who was he under that mask? What did his threat mean? And why did he make it?

Bat-Binoculars scanned the rooftops for long minutes, but to no avail. A man like that can be found only when he wants to be found . . . and that would no doubt happen when Batman least expected it.

His mind full of unanswered questions, Batman swung off, to be swallowed by the darkness.

Bane snorted derisively. He stood now on another roof, hundreds of yards away. "I thought you told me Batman was something special, Bird?"

A slim, blond man with his hair pulled back in a ponytail shrugged. "He is—at least as far as Gotham criminals are concerned." Bird stroked Talon, the sharp-beaked hawk that clung tightly to his other arm.

A moving spotlight beam briefly illuminated the other two members of Bane's gang. Zombie was tall and bald, his complexion sallow and unhealthy, while Trogg was built like a human bulldozer.

"Is it wise to take this chance?" Zombie asked. "Taunting Batman like that could jeopardize our whole mission!"

Bane turned to his minion. Even under the dark blue hood with the mysterious tubes and the zipper up the back, his menace could be felt. "I wanted one last look at my foe the way he is," he spat, "so noble and decent and sickeningly good . . . before I start to break him!"

Bane's hand reached around to the back of his neck, to a series of small tubes that disappeared under his hood—and were connected directly into the base of his skull. His finger touched a small control, and a precisely measured dose of liquid bubbled through the tubes.

Suddenly Bane threw his head back and let out a long, loud howl that echoed away across the rooftops. Even Bird, who'd known him longest and knew just how dangerous this man could be, had to suppress a shiver. Batman didn't stand a chance!

ARKHAM ASYLUM FOR THE CRIMINALLY INSANE.

Beyond a high wall, set well back in wooded grounds, stood the ivy-covered Victorian mansion that had been built to house Gotham's most dangerous lunatics.

A thin, piping cry issued from an open window as Mr. Zsasz, who carved a wound in his own flesh every time he slayed a victim, managed to attack an orderly. A brief shuffle, a full hypodermic, and the inhuman laugh faded.

Jeremiah Arkham, asylum governor and nephew of the original founder, was grateful. When one patient was unsettled, it tended to upset the others, too. Maybe now they'd get a quiet night.

Outside there was a sudden roaring. Jeremiah, passing a barred window, caught a glimpse of orange flame, then was hurled back in a shower of shattered glass as a huge explosion blew the window in around him. The building shook, and acrid smoke filled the corridors as more fierce blasts rang out.

"All security cells breached!" the speaker system blared. "The inmates are loose!"

On a small rise overlooking the asylum, Bane

gave a grunt of satisfaction as he lowered the mobile missile launcher. "Give Zombie the signal!"

Above them a small helicopter swooped into view, Zombie steering it on a course directly above the asylum. The blaze was spreading to the roof now; shadowy figures ran around in confusion.

Zombie laughed cruelly. "Now, Trogg!"

The bull-man opened the chopper hatch and sent a half dozen wooden crates crashing groundward. Yelling inmates jumped aside as the crates burst in the ruins below, weaponry scattering on the ground.

A criminal known as Cornelius Stirk bent to lift a rifle, a manic grin on his disfigured face. He turned to his companions, their numbers now swollen to at least thirty, with more arriving every minute. "Someone seems to be giving us a second chance, gentlemen." He gestured to the weapons lying on the ground and laughed. "Let's not waste it!"

The police were met by a murderous hail of lead.

Bane felt pleased as they sped down the hill, heading back to their base in the city. Almost every one of Batman's foes had been held in Arkham; now they—and dozens like them—were free to prey on Gotham to their hearts' content. Of course Batman would try to stop them . . . and it was there Bane's fun would really begin.

# Two

**E**ven in daylight Gotham City is a sinister place. Towering buildings cast unnatural shadows on the concrete canyons far below. Though they say only tourists look up, almost every skyscraping tower has its own external decoration. Some boast huge marble Greek gods and Roman emperors, while others sport Art Deco carvings. And gargoyles . . . everywhere you look there are gargoyles.

Bruce Wayne settled down in the back of his limousine as it pulled away from Wayne Tower, hub of the vast network of companies and charities that billionaire Wayne controlled, and joined the slow-moving afternoon traffic.

Alfred Pennyworth, Wayne's English butler and oldest friend, was at the wheel. "The meeting regarding the foundation's annual accounts is scheduled for six o'clock, sir."

Bruce sighed. To a casual observer, he seemed to typify the role he filled—tall, in his early thirties, well dressed and good-looking. A wealthy young man whose reputed playboy ways didn't sit easily with his vast commercial responsibilities. "I have other business tonight, Alfred."

The chauffeur frowned. "They'll think, of course, that you're off having fun, living up to your playboy image. A great pity they can never know the truth."

They were out of the financial district now, leaving the gleaming glass and steel spires of the banks and corporations behind as Alfred headed for the freeway out of town, skirting the slums that ringed the city and spread out from it like cancerous growths.

A few miles later, an exit ramp led onto a small road winding higher into wooded hills. This was the turf of Gotham's elite, the superrich, mansions and estates established by the great nineteenth century industrial barons.

Alfred chose a narrow turnoff, slowed, and swung out to pass a lone cyclist on a lightweight mountain bike. As they passed, Alfred hit the horn, and the fresh-faced teenage rider threw them a wave.

The driveway behind the wrought iron security gates was almost a quarter of a mile long, curving through grassland studded with beech and elm. At the end of it sat Wayne Manor, where the family had lived for generations. Bruce was the only surviving member of his line, and now the big house was empty except for him and his faithful, aging butler.

The two hurried up the front stairs and through the thick oak door. The hall was thirty feet long, lined with portraits of illustrious Wayne ancestors. At the far end a broad wooden staircase swept up to the first and second floors. Against the wall close by stood an old grandfather clock, its deep bass tick the loudest sound in the hall.

Standing before it, Bruce reached up, opening the glass that covered the face.

"If I may be so bold, Master Bruce," Alfred began, "I'm sure a short nap wouldn't go amiss—you haven't slept at all in twenty-four hours!"

"No time, Alfred. Things are far too serious!" Bruce was swiveling the clock's iron hands with one finger. Silently, a section of wall at the rear of the clock case slid away, revealing a small, dark opening.

The secret passage opened onto a flight of stairs, which in turn led down to a vast system of natural caves and tunnels that underlay the mansion. As Bruce walked down the steps, dim lights flicked on automatically.

He paused at a dark recess, quickly peeling off his clothes and replacing them with the costume that hung there.

When he emerged into the cave, a black cowl covered half his face, the eyeholes little more than slits. The cape that hung from his shoulders was long and voluminous but ultralight. Beneath it he wore a skintight gray costume and yellow belt. Gauntlets covered his hands and wrists, and tight-fitting boots came up to his knees. In the center of his chest shone a golden oval, imprinted with the stylized silhouette of a bat.

A secret known to a select few, Bruce Wayne's role as billionaire playboy was merely an act, a clever decoy to deflect attention from his real life's work—protecting Gotham City as the Batman.

The Batcave was the size of a football field. In the dim glow could be seen several of the trophies Batman kept as mementos of some of his stranger cases—a life-size *Tyrannosaurus rex,* a giant penny, a glass case containing the costume that once belonged to his partner Jason Todd, alias Robin, the Boy Wonder.

Cocky and aggressive, Jason had been the second Robin, successor to Dick Grayson. Even Boy Wonders grow up and look for a life of their own, and Dick had gone off to forge a new identity for himself as Nightwing, costumed leader of the super-hero group known as the Teen Titans.

Jason had seemed the perfect choice to follow Dick in the red, green, and gold costume. But the boy had made a fatal error of judgment and paid for it with his life. Batman had vowed then never again to work with a partner and assume the responsibility for anyone other than himself.

*Some vow!* he thought now. *Look where it's got me!*

Bruce stepped toward the monitors and the sophisticated computer equipment that flanked them—the mighty twin Cray supercomputers that formed the heart of his crime-fighting empire. Images and data darted continually across their flickering screens.

He'd spent the remainder of last night at Arkham Asylum, combing the woods and surrounding countryside, trying to round up as many escaped felons as he could before they split up and found their way back into Gotham. He'd recaptured at least half a dozen single-handed, but more than thirty had got clean away, including all of the major villains. Their names and images flashed on his screens now: the Joker, Two-Face, Scarecrow, Poison Ivy, Mad Hatter, Cornelius Stirk, Mr. Zsasz, Ventriloquist and his dummy Scarface, Killer Croc, Abattoir, Film

Freak, Amygdala, the Cavalier, Firefly . . . every one of them a brilliant yet insane criminal.

"Makes for some grim reading, doesn't it, partner?"

Batman turned to face the fourteen-year-old boy who wore the slick costume and narrow eye mask that proclaimed him as Robin . . . the boy his limo had passed earlier on the road.

Yes, he'd vowed there wouldn't be a third Robin. But Timothy Drake was too good, too smart to pass up; besides, the boy just wouldn't take no for an answer. Batman had tested him exhaustively before allowing him out onto the streets. The last thing he wanted was a repetition of the nightmare of Jason's death.

Quickly, Batman explained what had happened the night before—how he'd been taunted by the mysterious Bane, then a half hour later called to the biggest breakout in the asylum's history.

"You think it was this Bane who busted them out?" Robin asked doubtfully.

"Too much of a coincidence for it not to be!"

A monitor screen flashed. ROBBERY—HABER-DASHERY ON SALEM STREET!

"Come on," Batman said curtly, heading into the far darkness of the Cave. Robin followed.

A spotlight flared, illuminating the auto bay and the incredible, jet-black machine that filled it. Sliding into the driver's side, pulling down the heavy gull wing door after him, Batman fired the Batmobile's mighty V12 engine into life as Robin strapped himself into the passenger seat.

The Batmobile shot forward, pressing Robin back hard against his seat. Its headlights flared, lighting the seemingly blank wall of the cave ahead. They raced straight at it with ever-increasing speed, and electronic sensors slid the concealed exit swiftly open. Then they were out into the night air, picking up speed as Batman steered down a narrow hidden track.

Miniature hologram projectors buried in the ground cast a convincing image of a thorn- and shrub-choked rock face. No one would ever guess the secret that lay behind it.

"Okay, I give up," Robin said. "What's a haberdashery?"

"A fancy name for a hat shop." Batman looked ahead to where the twinkling lights of Gotham could be seen. "It's my bet that's where we'll find Jervis Tetch!"

Robinson Park had long since closed for the night, but it was far from empty. Overshadowed by the large bronze statue of Alice in Wonderland in the park's center, a long table had been set up. A large teapot stood on it, and at each of the ten places that were set was a cup and saucer. Beside each cup lay a hat stolen from the haberdashery.

Eight of the Arkham escapees were seated there, obviously unhappy about being out in the open. One of them turned to the man at the head of the table. "What's the big idea, Tetch? Why did you invite us all here?"

Jervis Tetch was a small, plump man in a long, bottle green frock coat and matching top hat, a dead ringer for his namesake, the Mad Hatter, in the Alice stories. "To attend my party, of course," he said brightly.

"I ain't putting on no stupid hat," one of the men began, but broke off abruptly as he found himself staring into the muzzle of a submachine gun wielded by Tetch.

Nervously, they picked up the hats and put them on—a trilby here, a fedora there, a hunting cap, a Stetson.

"Each headpiece contains a miniature electronic Trance Inducer," Tetch purred. "While you wear them, you will be totally obedient to me. Now—" He picked up the teapot and started to pour. "Why don't we all have a nice cup of tea until the Batman finds the invitation I left him?"

From the shadows under a stand of trees, two figures watched.

"All of them are armed," Robin whispered. "This isn't going to be easy for us!"

"It'll be easy for you," Batman replied. "You're too inexperienced to be going up against guns. Stay here. Provide backup if I need it."

Without waiting for a reply, Batman moved off, making no more sound than a shadow. The corners of Robin's mouth turned down huffily, but he knew better than to argue.

The thugs at the table sat still and expressionless, entranced by the powerful circuitry fitted into each hat. But the Mad Hatter's ridiculous face darkened as he saw the silhouette of his most hated foe.

"Now!" he yelled to his minions. "Kill him now!"

Eight guns spoke as one, beating out a rhythmic tattoo of death. But their target had already melted silently into the surrounding shadows, so while lead blasted through the branches and ricocheted off the bronze statue, it never came near Batman.

"Fools! I put you under my command so there wouldn't be any foul-ups! Spray the whole area!"

The eight men rose to their feet in unison, loosing off shots in all directions. No way even the accursed Batman could escape that!

But ten feet up, in the branches of a tree, Batman's mouth pursed grimly. He had to put a stop to this—now! In quick succession three Batarangs spun from his hand, their heavy weighted tips connecting with their targets; three men collapsed unconscious.

Robin had dived behind a stout trunk as soon as the shooting started. Now he cautiously poked his head out, just in time to see the jagged-edged shadow of Batman drop from the tree, landing lightly in the center of the table. The Hatter screamed and pointed—but too late.

Batman in action was a joy to watch, his every move calculated, his every blow dealt to gain maximum effect. The gunmen fell like ninepins before him.

"Imbeciles!" The Mad Hatter raised his machine gun. "Do I have to do everything myself?"

Batman had his back to Tetch, taking out the final thug as the Mad Hatter aimed the gun.

"So long, Bat-freak," he whispered—then grunted in pain and careened forward as Robin rammed into his back. He whirled, surprisingly fast for such a ridiculous figure, gun pointed at the boy.

But before he could shoot, a swinging foot sent the gun flying. "So long yourself," Batman said, and his fist exploded against the Hatter's chin.

Head bowed, Robin watched as Batman stooped to tie the unconscious thugs with Batline, enough to hold them until the police arrived. He knew he'd been wrong to disobey, even if it had been with the best of intentions.

"I couldn't just let Tetch shoot you!" he protested, when Batman had finished.

"I saw him," Batman said simply. "I'd already figured out how to take him myself."

"I'm sorry," the teenager apologized in a low voice. Batman looked intently at him, and for an instant Robin thought he saw a great weariness in his mentor's eyes. But his heart sank at Batman's next words.

"I refuse to imperil you further, Robin. The Arkham escapees are just too dangerous for you to tackle. Until they're caught, I'm taking you off active duty!"

# Three

The Bates Hotel was a dingy, run-down place, where service was nonexistent and as long as the bills were paid, nobody asked any questions.

In a shabby room Bane's gang sat watching TV. They'd been cooped up here since they engineered the Arkham breakout, and Trogg, Bird, and Zombie were getting restless.

As for Bane—he just sat, brooding, on what had been, and what was still to come.

A news announcer appeared on-screen. "Police have just announced the capture of the Mad Hatter and eight other Arkham escapees . . ."

Trogg made a gesture of contempt. "We could take Batman easy—any one of us! I don't understand why you play this waiting game, Bane!"

"Because it pleases me," Bane said softly. "We

rotted years in jail before we could put my plans into action. I am in no hurry.''

The four had first met while in Peña Duro prison on the Caribbean island of Santa Prisca, where Bane had been born. Under the island's medieval laws, the baby was charged with the crimes of his father—so he was born to life, and a life sentence, behind the walls of the ''Hard Stone.''

After his mother's death, the nameless child was left to fend for himself among the other convicts. For the first years of his life, the boy was coached by the dregs of the earth—murderers, arsonists, and thieves. The dank and gloomy corridors of the impregnable fortress-jail were his nursery. He learned how to cheat and steal and fight, because in that terrible human sink only the strong survived.

When El Jefe, the jail's cruel governor, had him tortured for fighting, the youth never flinched. Pain only made him tougher.

He vowed someday he would become the bane of his enemies' lives . . . and so he was named: Bane!

A mile across town, a bizarre figure was tied to a streetlight.

''I'll get you, Batman!'' he screeched, as a jagged-edged patch of darkness swung away from him into the night. ''One day I'll have you at my mercy! I'll eat your stinking heart!''

Cornelius Stirk was a major catch, a serial killer who'd brutalized over a dozen victims. A complete stroke of luck that Batman had spotted him lurking outside an apartment building. Usually catching evildoers was a matter of detective skills and sheer hard work.

The night sky lit up as a searchlight probed it, projecting a large yellow oval with the familiar bat silhouette on the underside of a cloud. Gotham's Police Commissioner Gordon needed to see him!

"Hit me, Bird!"

From a satchel resting against the wall, Bird took a small clear plastic tube filled with a dark liquid. Bane bent his head slightly, and Bird did something to the cluster of tubes at the base of his neck. He lifted away an empty tube and replaced it with a full one.

Bane lifted one hand, encased in a studded black gauntlet. One finger hovered over a button. There was a gentle swish, and liquid disappeared into the tube that ran under his hood and into his neck.

Incandescent power seemed to surge in him as the drug named Venom swept through his bloodstream. He felt invincible, unstoppable, filled with supreme, aggressive confidence.

When El Jefe had found he couldn't break Bane by normal means, he decided to try something even grislier. The Santa Priscan military had developed a new drug in their attempt to create a supersoldier, using the prison's inmates as their human guinea pigs. So far all the men tested had died. Now, El Jefe gave them Bane.

Based on the steroids used by some athletes, Venom was a concentrated derivative that packed a kick like a jackhammer. Almost overnight Bane's muscles swelled, and his strength and power grew out of proportion. But unlike the other unwilling test subjects, his heart didn't burst under the stress.

He used to sit in the cell he shared with the ex-Gothamite, Bird, and listen to the stories the blond man told. Stories of a mighty city, of unbelievable wealth. Stories of Gotham's criminals, its Arkham Asylum—and its Batman.

That was the part Bane loved most. Tales of the Batman, the Dark Knight, so noble and righteous as he waged his war on the city's crime.

This Batman had what Bane had never known—freedom. Locked in that dim cell, its damp walls covered in moss, rats shuffling around his feet, Bane swore everything would change.

He would go free—to Gotham! And once there he would hunt down this miraculous Batman and destroy everything about him.

•    •    •

Commissioner James Gordon sighed.

The majority of the Arkham escapees were still on the loose; at least thirty recent murders could be traced directly to them, and he knew that the deadly toll would continue to mount until they were all safely behind bars again.

He stood by a large, old-fashioned searchlight in a corner of the police department building's flat roof. It was this that cast the Bat-signal upward. It wasn't officially sanctioned, of course, this liaison between police commissioner and vigilante, because technically Batman was a criminal working outside the law. But the Darknight Detective and the policeman had helped each other many times over the years. They were both soldiers in the same war.

"You have information for me?"

Gordon should have been used to these silent entrances by now, but they always took him by surprise.

"Sewer worker claims he saw Killer Croc in the tunnels under Sixth Avenue." Gordon came right to the point. Neither of them had any time to waste. "Trouble is, every available unit's tied up."

"I'll do what I can."

Gordon glanced out at the Gotham nightscape. Strange how beautiful it looked, he thought, even to him, who knew the sordid reality behind the glittering facade.

When he turned around, Batman was gone.

Thick curtains covered the apartment window.

Inside, a young man with sculpted muscles was hefting a dumbbell, lifting the heavy bar with seemingly no effort. His blond hair was worn slightly long, and there was something about his clean good looks that hinted at a solitary, studious nature. Beside him, the smaller and slighter Robin was working out with weights half the size.

"I'm worried about him, Paul," the teenager said. "He's pushing himself too hard—going without sleep, taking on one foe after another without recharging his batteries in between!"

Jean Paul Valley exhaled and lowered the iron discs. "He's the boss, Robin," he said, his all-American voice belying the French name. "You and I are new to the hero game. It makes sense to do as he tells us, train until he feels we are ready."

"I'd never question his authority. It's just . . . I have this terrible feeling that he's going to need us!"

A single bead of perspiration ran down Paul's face. "Then we'd better make sure we're ready!"

Paul had been a computer student at Gotham University—until the day his father staggered home covered in blood and dying. It had seemed like a nightmare as Paul listened to his tale. His father had a secret identity—he was also Azrael, the Avenging

Angel, who punished rule-breaking members of the ancient and secret Order of St. Dumas.

"The order split off from the Knights Templar in the fourteenth century," the dying man explained, "and over the years became fabulously wealthy. But recently a man called LeHah—our treasurer's son—started to loot the order's riches. As Azrael, it was my duty to challenge him and bring him to justice. I . . . I have failed!"

The role of Azrael had been handed down from father to son for six hundred years. Paul was horrified to discover that *he* was now expected to put on the robes and mask of office, to pick up and brandish the fiery sword of death.

"I can't!" he'd protested. "I'm a student. I don't know anything about fighting!"

But even that wasn't true. Since Paul's babyhood, his father had been hypnotically indoctrinating him every night of his life with the secrets of the System. Although he had never consciously learned any of it, Paul soon discovered that his father's words were true—he had instinctive knowledge of almost every technique an assassin was likely to need. He couldn't call on it when he wanted, but instead had to wait for the System to spring into use—usually at moments of extreme stress.

Paul's path crossed that of the Dark Knight when Batman was investigating the order, and though at first they seemed on different sides, they ended up as allies. When Paul saved Batman's life, Batman saw the potential the younger man held as a crime fighter. The System, though little understood, made Paul a force to be reckoned with, and so Batman had set him a rigorous training schedule to prepare him for his place in the never-ending war.

Now Paul's eyes were grim. Batman had helped him when he needed it most. If the situation were reversed, Paul wouldn't let him down.

The stench in the sewers was almost unbearable, but Killer Croc didn't mind. He'd lived down here on and off for years, away from the city and the citizens he hated, and had grown used to its foulness.

His eyes had adjusted well to the darkness, and he could see where other men would be blind. The crumbling brick tunnel curved away in front of him. Here and there a pipe gushed out waste, the sound echoing into the distance.

Killer Croc was a big man, six and a half feet and muscled like the pro wrestler he once had been. He'd worked the fairgrounds all over America, the county shows and the rodeos, taking on all comers, any style they liked. Since childhood he'd suffered from a raging skin disease that turned the outer layers of his flesh into a hard, shell-like covering. In the ring he was a fearsome sight.

And he had never once been beaten . . . until he came to Gotham, turned his talents to crime—and met up with the Batman.

Ahead, the tunnel branched. His craggy brow knitted over cruel, piglike eyes. This was a great place for an ambush.

Less than twenty yards away, crouched on a ledge at the start of one of the subtunnels, Batman held his breath. Not hard, in this stench, though the nose filter he wore cut out most of the offensive odors.

Through the infrared visor that covered the eye slits in his cowl, he watched Killer Croc. Slowly, so slowly it was barely perceptible, his hand stole to his utility belt.

Killer Croc heard the sharp sound of something being flicked.

"Batman!" he yelled. "I see ya!"

Fury exploded inside him. Croc loved nothing more than a fight! He balled his fists, started angrily forward—and halted abruptly as a phosphor flare burst in the air. White light burned against his eyeballs and he staggered back, hands to his face, blinded.

Batman's fists shot out, one-two, one-two, taking

the man squarely on the jaw. It hardly seemed to faze him. Killer Croc was one of the strongest, meanest foes he'd ever faced; the fact that he'd defeated him in the past meant nothing.

Then Croc was fighting back, fists pummeling blindly, blows crashing into Batman's shoulder and upper arm. Batman rolled away, muscles momentarily numbed, only for Killer Croc to land another blow from behind. His brawny arms closed around Batman's waist and wrestled him to the ground.

"Now who's laughin', big shot?" Croc demanded, his vision returning. "I'm gonna beat you within an inch of your interferin' life!"

Batman grunted as a fist took him twice on his unprotected head. He knew he couldn't take many more of these awful blows. Desperately he twisted, his hand wrenching at a pocket on his utility belt. It was all over, unless—

His fingers closed around a small plastic sphere, pulling it free. Suddenly he let his body relax. Taken off guard, Killer Croc toppled forward—and Batman crushed the sphere under Croc's nose.

The big man fell to his knees, gagging as the potent knockout gas did its work.

"I'll get ya . . . one day . . . I'll get ya!" His voice trailed off, and he keeled over, unconscious.

•    •    •

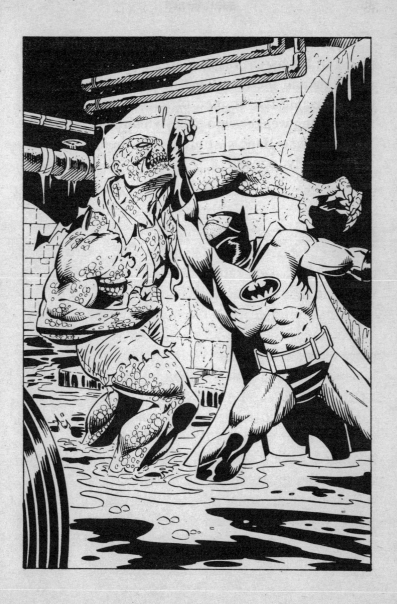

For a long minute, Batman didn't even move. The sound of his harsh, rasping breath drowned out the splashing and the rats. That had been close—much too close. He felt drained of all strength and emotion, getting weaker with every villain that he faced.

If that was Bane's strategy, he thought, it was working only too well.

# Four

A week passed, seven long nights in which Batman was stretched to his fullest capacity, seven too-short days in which he never seemed to have enough time to rest and recover.

He'd achieved much: captured the dangerous swordsman the Cavalier, the man-brute Amygdala, and two or three others, as well as foiling a major plot against the city by Two-Face, the insane former District Attorney.

It wasn't enough. Every minute the escaped inmates remained at liberty spelled danger for Gotham's people. *His* people.

Now, on a Friday afternoon, dark clouds scudded across the sun, dappling Wayne Manor in light and shade. A storm was building.

•  •  •

"Shondra! Hi!" Bruce Wayne had slept for only three hours, yet he was careful to keep the discomfort from his voice. He'd taken some bad knocks, was sporting bruises on bruises, feeling far from his best. "How can I help?"

"By keeping your appointments with your doctor!" The pleasant female voice at the other end of the telephone line had a hard edge. "You were due in my office an hour ago!"

"Shondra, I'm sorry. It was . . . pressure of business." This was the only part of his double life that he hated—the fact that in order to preserve his secret identity, he sometimes had to lie to people he liked.

Her voice softened. "Bruce, you're in an extremely high-stress job. You need to learn how to relax—and my techniques can help you."

*If only you knew!* Bruce thought. Shondra Kinsolving was a much sought after practitioner of alternative medicine, who used her own natural healing abilities on her patients to good effect. Tim Drake's invalid father, Jack, had improved miraculously since she'd started treating him.

"I'm next door at the Drake place now," Shondra was saying. "I could be with you in five minutes."

"Sorry," Bruce replied—and he genuinely was. "I have some research to do. But I'll see you tonight at the Grand Charity Dinner."

"You're taking the night off?" Alfred inquired as Bruce hung up, unable to keep the pleasure out of his voice. "I'm glad. You need a rest."

"Well." Bruce looked a little guilty. "I have a hunch the charity show's going to be robbed!"

Sixteen-year-old Orson Zeen finished his handiwork with a flourish and took three steps back, the better to admire the glowing six-inch-high graffiti.

His two companions, who'd been keeping watch at either end of the alley, grinned. "Yo, O! Now everybody's gonna know about the Bad Boys gang!"

"Afraid not, guys."

Standing on the lip of a low roof ten feet above their heads were two imposing figures, both wearing costumes and capes.

"Wh-what do you want with us?" Orson stammered.

"I want you to clean it up." Paul's voice was low and measured, with just a hint of a threat. "We'll be back in an hour. If it's not done, we'll come looking for you."

Orson was losing face. How could he expect to be a gang leader if he let creeps like this dictate to him? "Kiss it!" he snapped, almost surprised at his own boldness. "Why should we do what *you* tell us?"

"Because you're breaking the law—" Robin started, but broke off as Paul abruptly swung down to the ground.

Breathing heavily under his hood, Paul grabbed the front of the startled gang leader's shirt in a bunch. "Because I'll hurt you if you don't!" Paul snarled. He turned away without another word. He and Robin disappeared, leaving three frightened Bad Boys wondering where they could get a scrubbing brush at this time of night.

"That was heavy," Robin remarked as they swung together over the chasm between two office blocks. Their long hours of practice had started to hone them into a team . . . and now Paul had to go and spoil it with his harsh actions.

"They're trash," Paul replied matter-of-factly. "Fear is the only way to teach them anything!"

He soared twenty feet down through the air and landed lightly on a roof. "I hope Batman cuts us loose real soon. All this training's getting boring. I'm ready for some genuine action!"

Robin followed. Paul's outburst against the Bad Boys gang was uncalled for, a sign of weakness. Robin couldn't help wondering: *Was that really Paul speaking . . . or was it Azrael, the role of Avenging Angel that the System had planted in his mind?*

•  •  •

The clouds had piled up, thick and dark.

Tonight was the biggest charity event of the year. The sculpted Gothic columns that flanked the entry to the Civic Center were bathed in muted lights. Limos pulled up one after the other, disgorging the city's rich and famous.

Inside, in the banqueting room, Bruce Wayne sipped a tonic water, politely nodding to the new arrivals, shaking hands, kissing the occasional cheek. But his eyes were never still, casting around, looking for clues. Elaborate flower arrangements graced each white-draped table. A large banner read: $1,000,000 CASH!

This was the night the huge cash collection, all in neat stacks of one-thousand-dollar bills, would be handed over to the security firm working for Dr. Leslie Thompkins, head of a fund that provided free clinics for Gotham's poor and disadvantaged. It was a magnet for any thief.

Bruce stared at the woman in charge of security, issuing orders to her four burly uniformed men. *Now where have I seen her before?* he wondered.

"Bruce! You look absolutely awful!" came a voice from behind him.

It was Dr. Shondra Kinsolving. Tall, slim, and very pretty, she looked anything but happy. "I'd swear you hadn't slept for a week!"

Murmuring some feeble excuse, Bruce led her to their table.

On a rooftop directly across the street, Bane lowered the powerful binoculars from his eyes. From where he stood he had a perfect view through the plate glass windows into the chamber where the charity dinner had started.

"Bruce Wayne," Bane said flatly, "is the man we have been taunting. Bruce Wayne is Batman!"

Bird sneered. "That rich geek? You must be joking!"

"I never joke." The smile vanished from the other man's face. "We have been watching Batman for weeks. I know him. Wayne's body language— the way he moves, the way he holds his head—is the same. He is Batman . . . and we have learned his greatest secret!"

Trogg smacked a football-sized fist into his open palm. "You mean—we get to hurt him now?"

Like an omen, the first flash of lightning streaked jaggedly across the sky, and the storm broke.

Dinner had ended, and Leslie Thompkins was halfway through her acceptance speech.

Was it Bruce's imagination, or was it awfully warm in here? He felt light-headed. It couldn't have been the brandy the waiters had served; he never touched alcohol.

He glanced at Shondra and saw she was sitting with her head in her hands, her eyes half closed and drooping. Behind her, other diners looked in the same state. Only the security people seemed unaffected.

*Something's wrong,* Bruce thought, and then: *Of course! The flowers! It's gas from the flowers!*

Pulling a small nose filter from inside his shirt, he inserted it and waited for his head to clear. He guessed at once who was behind this—Poison Ivy, a beautiful botanist who used her talent with plants to poison and steal.

Bruce let himself slip forward in his chair. None of the guards looked his way. Surreptitiously, he slid beneath the tablecloths that reached almost to the floor. Whatever happened next, it wouldn't be as Bruce Wayne that he'd face it.

The young woman who'd been in charge grasped the wig she was wearing and pulled it off, allowing her natural red hair to tumble free. She also peeled off the suit she wore, revealing a skintight green costume underneath. Poison Ivy had once been a law-abiding botanist. But an experiment that went wrong had warped her nature and poisoned her very blood.

She stepped up onto the podium and addressed

the entranced gathering. "Everybody stand up. Put all your jewelry, cash, and credit cards on the table in front of you!"

Her tinkling laughter cut across the room as in unison fifty chairs scraped back.

Suddenly the lights went out, plunging them into pitch darkness.

By the time Ivy found the light switch, her cohorts lay dazed and bound, and a grim Batman faced her.

She smiled and walked toward him, her arms out as if she were greeting an old flame. His head felt heavy, it was getting hard for him to focus. Her perfume . . . there was something about her perfume.

She stood on tiptoe, pursing her lips. "You're under my spell—my willing slave. Kiss me!"

No! He couldn't let her kiss him—the toxins that raged through her bloodstream were fatal to others, and she spread them via her deadly lips.

Summoning all his willpower, Batman made one final desperate effort, pushing her roughly away. The spell was broken. Ivy ran—but Batman's triple-weighted bola whipped through the air, wrapping itself around her ankles, bringing her to the floor.

Batman's body was one aching mass as he left the Civic Center by the rear door and clambered to the roof. Already he could hear the sirens as police and ambulances rushed through the rain.

He sat down in the shelter of a large air-conditioning unit, sucking in wet air, seeking a moment of respite in the midst of all this violence.

And suddenly the world exploded as a crashing blow struck the back of his head. Instinct sent him rolling forward, flipping in a complete somersault. He twisted upon landing to face his attacker.

"Bane sent me," Trogg giggled, and it was an ugly sound. "He says I can hurt you."

He gave a roar like a bull and lumbered forward—but this time Batman was ready. "Bane might say you can—but I don't!" he snapped. Falling back under Trogg's charge, Batman brought up his legs as his back hit the roof. His feet took Trogg in the chest, and he straightened his legs with as much power as he could muster.

Trogg let out a startled cry as he flew over Batman's head, flailing through the air to hit the concrete parapet, where he slumped unconscious.

Batman caught a movement out of the corner of his eye. A knife!

He leapt aside just in time. Three six-inch blades whistled through the air and struck stone only inches behind him.

"Trogg is a mere brute," Zombie said, as he stepped out from the shadows where he'd been crouched. "But I am a master craftsman in the ways of the blade!"

It was hard to make Batman out through the driving rain, but he could see the cape flapping in the wind. "Die!" he screamed as he ran forward, the long dagger he held slicing through the air and into the cape's fabric.

Batman slugged him from behind. He'd slipped out of his cape and lashed it roughly to a TV aerial, while he waited behind the box of the air conditioner.

Batman picked up the cape. He was breathing hard now, but he heard the whoosh of the hawk's wings as it dived down at him, talons raking for his face. He ducked, brought the cape up, and ensnared the bird in one fluent movement. He dropped it as the third of Bane's henchmen came spinning out of the darkness.

"You're tired, old man!" Bird spun on one foot, the other slamming into Batman's chest with bone-jarring force. "Why not just lie down and accept that you're beat?"

But that was something Batman would never admit. Bird was a karate expert, but Batman had trained with the very best and knew moves the other had never even heard of. Weak and weary as he was, adrenaline and instinct were enough, and Bird soon lay unconscious with the others.

· · ·

Twelve minutes later Batman was parked in the Batcave's auto bay. His muscles were beginning to stiffen, and he could taste blood at the back of his mouth. His ribs were throbbing, his head aching from the fight.

He staggered upstairs, clutching at the cold cave wall for support.

Emerging from the secret entrance behind the clock, he knew at once something was wrong. Ornaments lay smashed on the floor, and a table was overturned.

"Alfred . . . ?" His voice was tinged with anxiety.

The aged butler lay sprawled, unmoving, on an Oriental rug. His eyes were closed, and blood trickled from a fast-swelling bruise on his forehead.

And standing there was Bane, waiting.

# Five

Outside Wayne Manor, an angry streak of lightning split the air, the bright flash throwing everything in the room into sharp relief.

"Why?" Batman asked between gritted teeth. "Why do you hate me so much that you would do this?"

"Because you have something I want," Bane sneered. "Gotham City." He cracked his knuckles, and it sounded like a gunshot. "And tonight, it will be mine!"

Batman was drinking in every detail, every last visual fact that he could learn about his enemy. Information is power. Bane was fresh, in peak physical condition—while Batman himself was almost at the end of his tether.

*I have to take the fight to him—*

Without further ado he pirouetted on one foot, the other shooting out and up, driving like a piston into Bane's ribs. The bigger man hadn't expected the attack. Despite his strength and weight he tottered back—and grunted twice as Batman's elbow smashed into the side of his head.

But he laughed. "The Arkham inmates performed their task well, Batman. You are no match for me under normal conditions. Weak and tired, you will be a pushover!"

"You talk too much!" Batman slithered away as Bane made a swift grab for him. Irritated by his failure, Bane snatched up a heavy bronze vase and hurled it with fierce intent. Batman dived aside and the vase crashed into an ornate glass-fronted display cabinet. Expensive porcelain shattered into a thousand fragments.

Rolling forward, Batman somersaulted. As he straightened, his foot caught Bane behind the ankles and brought him heavily to the flagstone floor. They wrestled for a moment, straining against each other, neither able to gain the advantage.

"You are stronger than I gave you credit for," Bane grunted, "but that will only prolong your agony!"

*Strange,* Batman thought. Only minutes ago he

was bushed, ready to call it a day. Yet here he was fighting as if nothing had ever happened to him. He knew it couldn't last. This was his body's final push.

Batman flexed his legs, and a well-aimed kick knocked Bane flying into one of the suits of medieval armor at the base of the stairway. Man and armor fell together.

About to follow through, Batman paused. Alfred had struggled to his hands and knees, looking hurt and confused and very, very old.

"Get out, Alfred! Hurry! Go!"

The faithful servant didn't want to leave his master alone with this monster, but he knew there was nothing he could do here.

As Alfred hobbled toward the front door, Batman leapt back to the fray, his fists pounding into Bane. He was doing well, hadn't taken one decent blow. Maybe he was going to come out of this all right after all—

Then Bane struck back. He'd absorbed Batman's blows, a tribute to the long years he'd spent in Peña Duro's extreme conditions. But now it was his turn.

Bane's arms opened wide and he brought both fists slamming down together on Batman's head with crushing force. Batman stopped dead, the blow resonating all the way down his body to his feet.

Bane's piercing red eyes seemed to glitter with hatred beneath his hood. "The sparring is over. Now we fight for real!"

He moved forward with incredible speed, snatching Batman in a rib-cracking bear hug.

Just then all of Batman's tiredness came flooding back in a tidal wave. He was closer to total exhaustion than he'd ever been. He felt like just closing his eyes and drifting off into blackness . . .

But something inside wouldn't let him. "That's not what being a hero's all about," it seemed to say. "You took a vow to protect the people of Gotham. If ever they needed you, it's now—to stop this monster and his evil ambitions!"

A cry of pain and frustration and sheer rage boiled up inside him, bursting from his lips even as he burst from Bane's arms. He was the Batman; he would never give in!

He struck out, but Bane was far from finished and returned blow for blow. They clashed like titans until they both stood panting and gasping for breath. Then Bane lifted his glove and pressed a silver stud set in it.

"Venom," he hissed, "the wonder drug! Venom makes me the strongest man who ever lived!"

Bane felt so powerful he laughed aloud. His right arm shot out like a pile driver, crashing through Batman's guard like it wasn't there.

Batman must have passed out for a moment, for the next thing he knew Bane had hoisted him high over his head.

"Beg for mercy!" the criminal snarled. "Scream my name!"

Batman grimaced, hardly able to force out the words between his swollen lips. "G-go . . . back to . . . hell!"

And that was the final straw. "I am Bane. I could kill you—but death would only end your agony, and silence your shame. Instead, I will simply"—Bane brought Batman's helpless body slamming down over his knee—"break you!"

Red fire lanced through Batman's back, pain spasmed through his every nerve, then everything went black.

The storm had passed, and the house was silent. Even the clock had stopped ticking.

The creak of the door opening was a screech in the stillness.

Robin and Paul entered, alertly scanning the hall, ready if need be to face up to Bane. But he was gone.

Batman lay awkwardly, his body twisted at an unnatural angle. His face was pale and his breath shallow and ragged. Robin's heart sank. His partner—his mentor—his friend—lay broken like a rag

doll! Tears pricked the back of Robin's eyes, but he dashed them determinedly away. This was no time for sentiment. Batman was seriously hurt. This was time for decisive action.

"Paul—there's a stretcher in the kitchen cupboard. Get it!"

Paul hurried off, and Alfred entered. He'd gone straight to the Drake house when he fled and fortunately found Tim. The teenager's call found Paul working out in his garage, and they'd met up at the manor.

"He's badly hurt, Alfred," the teenager said, as the old retainer knelt by the broken body. "Stay with him, do what you can. I'll prepare the med-room!"

Batman had long lived with the knowledge that severe injury could befall him at any time. To have gone to a hospital would have meant exposing his secret identity, forever rendering him useless as a crime fighter. So he'd had a special room constructed in the manor's west wing, equipped with the very latest in medical technology, and made sure that Alfred and Tim were proficient in its use.

An hour later they'd done all they could. Bruce was resting peacefully, his breathing still shallow but regular now. His wounds were dressed, his body strapped into a special corset that relieved the pressure on his back. Fortunately, Tim's worst fear hadn't been realized—the spine wasn't broken.

Alfred sat by Bruce, his own injury forgotten. Nothing would have induced him to leave that bedside.

Eight hours later, when Bruce finally opened his eyes, Alfred still sat there.

Bruce opened his mouth to speak, but Alfred quickly shushed him. "Save your strength, sir." He knew there was no point in being evasive. The master wouldn't thank him for that. "You have sustained massive injuries. Broken ribs and arm, severe bruising to most of your body. I'm afraid the worst damage is to your back."

At the back of the room, Robin and Paul were silent.

Bruce's face was expressionless. "How . . . long?" he rasped.

"Until you're better, sir? My best estimate is months—perhaps years." Alfred paused again. He had hoped he would never have to say this. "Perhaps . . . never."

Bruce thought for a long, long moment. So he was finished as Batman! The reality of that fact didn't penetrate; it just seemed to be words. But he knew there was something he had to do.

"The package I once gave you," he said to Alfred. "Bring it. Then you and Robin leave me alone with Paul."

Years before, Bruce had given Alfred a sealed brown paper parcel and told him to keep it someplace safe until it was needed. That time was now.

When they were alone, Bruce held out the package to Paul.

Paul's mouth dropped and his eyes widened as he tore the paper away—revealing a Batman costume. "For me?" he asked in astonishment. "But why?"

"Because Gotham needs a protector and I can no longer fill the role. Because Robin's too young, and Nightwing has his own life with the Titans to live. Because as Azrael you impressed me. I trust you, Paul. I believe you can do it."

"I'm honored, Bruce. Truly honored!"

"There's only one condition," Bruce went on, staring hard into the other's eyes. "You can fight crime—but you must stay away from Bane. He's too dangerous for you. Do you promise?"

Paul nodded eagerly. To become the Batman, he'd have promised away his life. "Of course," he said. "Whatever you want. Me—the Batman? Wow! I won't let you down, Bruce—I swear!"

Bruce leaned back on his pillows and wearily closed his eyes. He'd done what was important, handed over the mantle of the Bat. "Take care . . . and take care of my city!"

# Part II

# KNIGHTQUEST:
## THE SEARCH AND THE CRUSADE

# One

One month later, everything was the same, yet everything was different.

Caught in a pool of light at the back of a downtown shopping mall, Batman and Robin were surrounded by weapon-wielding thugs they'd caught red-handed in a late-night heist. Three thugs were already down on the ground, in no condition to continue the fight; but another four were armed and willing.

The Dynamic Duo worked well together, covering each other's back, one ducking to allow the other to get in a cross-blow at their attackers. That's how it was the same.

The difference was, the man in the cape and cowl wasn't Bruce Wayne.

For thirty nights now, Jean Paul Valley had been

the Batman, and so far Robin could hardly fault the job he'd done. Paul was fast, strong, clever, and scary. Maybe even *too* scary.

Only one thug still stood, a bulky shaven-headed biker with a nose ring and tattoos. He held a metal bar, swinging it loosely.

"Put it down." Paul's voice was low and grating; he'd been practicing and could now sound exactly like Bruce used to. "Or I'll put *you* down."

Baldy gulped. He was no coward, but he wasn't crazy. The weapon dropped from his hand—only to be snatched by Batman before it hit the ground.

"Slime!" Batman snarled. "I ought to take this to you, the way you used it on the guard in the mall!"

"No!" Robin leapt forward, knocking the bar from his partner's hand. "That's not the way we do things!"

Batman let his victim go, and the man ran off, heading for the two police officers who were hurrying toward the sounds of commotion.

"I surrender!" he sobbed. "I'll tell you everything! Just don't let him get me!"

"Never look a gift horse in the mouth, Montoya." Officer Harvey Bullock glanced at his female companion as he pulled out his cuffs. "But tell me, fella—who's gonna get you?"

Montoya and Bullock followed the man's

trembling finger—but apart from six KO'd thugs, there was no one there at all.

"Don't ever do that to me again!"

The duo swung from building to building and landed on the third-floor platform of a fire escape.

"*I'm* Batman now," Paul continued. "We do things my way."

"What—beat up on a defenseless man who'd already surrendered?" Robin was outraged. "Bruce taught us to arrest criminals using minimum violence. If you think bullying and acting tough is what Batman is all about, then maybe Bruce made a mistake to appoint you as his successor!"

"So tell on me," Batman said coldly. He turned his back, gazing out on the neon-lit city that stretched away into the distance like the set of some science fiction movie. "There's a city out there that needs us. You can come with me—or if you don't like my methods, you can stay behind."

Without looking back, he launched himself into the air.

The Boy Wonder was not happy. He knew this was no way for Paul to be acting, and he wondered if he should tell Bruce. Robin brightened a little as he thought of the man he idolized. After his terrible defeat, Bruce's condition was improving daily. With the aid of his indomitable spirit he was now as mobile as a man in a wheelchair could be. But, it was still not known if he would walk again. Robin could only hope for the best.

The teenager turned and headed sadly for home.

Bane and his gang had moved up in the world from the dingy Bates Hotel. Their base of operations was now a penthouse in one of the city's most exclusive apartment blocks.

Bird laughed. He was seated on a plush leather armchair, the table beside him groaning under the weight of stacks of high-denomination bills. He tossed a handful in the air and laughed again as they fluttered down around him. "Gotta hand it to you, Bane—you're the greatest! From the highest roller to the lowest street punk, we get fifty cents on every crooked dollar that changes hands!"

"It is not just about money, Bird." Bane sat motionless; he'd been brooding again. "It is about power. Right now I control more than half of Gotham's illegal rackets. In another month, it will truly be *my* city!"

There was a short buzz, and he glanced at the security monitor screen. Trogg and Zombie stood outside the main entry, flanking a broad-shouldered, swarthy man in a pinstripe suit and fedora.

Bird punched in the combination that turned off the alarms and opened the steel-shuttered door.

Tough Tony Bressi strode forcefully into the room. "I have a complaint," Bane said quietly.

"*You* got a complaint?" Tough Tony was one of Gotham's major crime lords, and he wasn't used to being treated like this. "I gotta complaint! You're supposed to have crippled da Batman—"

"I did," Bane said with surprising vehemence.

"Yeah?" Tough Tony said with a sneer. "So how come he and his Boy Wonder dropped in on my guys when they were heistin' da mall earlier tonight?"

"He is an impostor!" Bane thundered. "I broke the Batman!"

"Impostor or not," Zombie said thoughtfully, "he seems to be doing a pretty good job. A lot of other gang bosses said the same thing when we picked up their dues."

"See?" Tough Tony sounded triumphant. "I ain't payin' no rake-off if you can't keep your part of the bargain!"

Bane stood, advancing slowly on the other man.

Bressi stood his ground. He'd worked his way up from street soldier, via hitman and debt collector, to crime lord. He didn't get where he was by backing down to guys like Bane.

Two minutes later he was cowering, bleeding and bruised, begging for Bane not to hit him again.

While Trogg and Zombie took Bressi out and dumped him in a cab home, Bane stood on the balcony, surveying the city of which he was soon going to be master. This new Batman had to be dealt with. He would find the new hero . . . and crush him!

The next day Bruce Wayne awoke feeling better than he had in a long time.

He missed being Batman and was disappointed that he had no choice but to break the vow he'd made to his parents all those years ago. But at the same time, he felt something akin to relief that the responsibility of Gotham's Guardian had passed from his shoulders.

He ignored the bell that would have summoned Alfred and swung himself out of bed into his wheelchair. With difficulty he dressed, then launched into the first of the exercise routines Dr. Kinsolving had given him. He felt bad that he'd lied to her about his injury; she thought he'd been in a high-speed car crash.

She'd been at his bedside daily while he recovered. Though her visits were purely professional at first, it wasn't long before they both realized how much they looked forward to each other's company.

Thirty minutes later Bruce took the elevator down to the ground floor and wheeled the chair down the ramp leading to the front drive. He knew Shondra had a morning appointment with Tim's father, Jack

Drake. He'd take the footpath through the woods and surprise her there.

Bruce pushed himself along the leafy path and up the slight slope, glorying in the morning sunshine.

He was almost at the edge of the shrubbery fronting the Drake place when he halted, sniffing the air. *Cigarette smoke! Strange. Who would be smoking here?*

He saw a figure in the shadows of a clump of leafy bushes. There was no mistaking the snub-nosed outline that jutted out from the man's arms . . . a submachine gun!

Bruce edged closer, silently willing the chair not to run over a dry twig and give him away. The man was wearing a ski mask, obviously standing guard. Beyond him, on the gravel drive outside the palatial home, a white truck with SPRANG FLOWERS painted garishly on the side was parked.

The house door opened, and another hooded man ran out. "Hurry!" he snapped, and Bruce could see two others exit behind him. One was dragging Shondra by her wrist, the other pushed along a protesting Jack Drake.

One of the thugs threw open the van's rear doors.

Bruce didn't stop to think. Snatching up a stout fallen branch, he wheeled himself vigorously forward. As the guard turned at the sound, Bruce

lashed out with the branch and took him hard on the chin.

"Stop!" Bruce yelled. "You can't take them! I won't let you!"

Two of the gun-wielding thugs ran at the newcomer. Bruce hit the first one in the solar plexus with the branch, doubling him up. But the other swung his rifle butt. There was a terrible crack, and Bruce's senses faded.

When Bruce came to, the thugs were gone. A black tide of despair swept through him. Only months ago he'd been the mighty Batman; the world's top criminals trembled when they heard his name. Now Bane had reduced him to this, a cripple lying on the grass beside his overturned wheelchair, a pathetic weakling who couldn't even save a woman and an old man.

Tim would be shocked to find his father kidnapped; how could Bruce face the teenager and tell him he'd failed . . . again? And Shondra—taken just when their friendship was on the point of becoming something more. He felt devastated.

And then that little voice inside him seemed to speak: "This isn't the way of the Batman."

The voice was right. So maybe he *was* crippled. So what? He'd always prided himself on being the World's Greatest Detective, hadn't he? His mind hadn't been affected by the cruel blows that broke his body.

He gritted his teeth. He would find Shondra and Jack, wherever their kidnappers had taken them!

# TWO

It was late afternoon when Tim returned home from school.

Usually his father was in the book-lined study at this time, but the room was empty. *Probably over at Bruce's or on an outing with Dr. Shondra,* he thought. Tim was secretly pleased.

He and Paul had unfinished business from last night. It was impossible to trust your life to someone you weren't even speaking to.

Unlocking a wooden hatch concealed under a kitchen rug, Tim hurried down the steps to the cellar. He changed into the Robin costume he kept hidden here and slid back a loose wall panel to reveal another opening. This was one he and Bruce had constructed. It connected with a series of small caves and passages and eventually ran into the Batcave.

Paul was in the cave now, in full costume apart from his cowl. Robin stepped out into the light and was surprised to see Paul holding both hands up in front of him. Instead of the normal Batman gloves, he was wearing a pair of fearsome high-tech gauntlets. Razor-edged "fins" decorated the gloves' sides, while the fingers ended in lethal-looking spikes.

"What the heck are those, Paul?"

"I . . . don't know. I just felt an urge to pick up pen and paper . . . then I fell into some sort of trance. When I came out of it, I had full designs for these things. I wondered if I could actually build them." He glanced admiringly at his handiwork. "They'll be invaluable! I'll be able to climb otherwise unscalable buildings—and make Batman's image that much more menacing!"

But Robin foresaw another use. "And cut throats, too!" he accused. "Batman always said we should rely on our minds and our wits—not weaponry." He broke off, unhappy. He'd come here for reconciliation, not another argument.

Paul was angry. "I'm Batman now! Me! I fight crime my way!"

His right gauntlet shot out suddenly, powering

through the air directly toward Robin's face. But the sharp, gleaming spikes stopped a centimeter short.

Paul's eyes blazed fiercely. "It seems we no longer agree, 'partner.' So why don't we just call it a day?"

Paul grabbed the teenager, and roughly propelled him toward the stairs. "Get out of this cave and don't come back!" He thrust Robin forward, almost stumbling. "I don't need a partner! From now on I work solo!"

Robin exited into the manor via the grandfather clock. He would have to tell Bruce about this. Maybe he should have confided in him earlier, but he hadn't wanted to burden him when his recuperation was what mattered.

The house was empty. Neither Bruce nor Alfred was anywhere to be found. Sadly, Robin headed for the front door—where he found a note pinned to it and addressed to him.

*Timothy*, it read. *Have faith. Master Bruce and I will find your father and his kidnappers. Take care of Paul.*

It was signed *Alfred*.

A small private WayneCorp jet taxied onto a peripheral runway at Gotham Airport.

Alfred, a qualified pilot, was at the controls, while

Bruce's chair was anchored to the floor in the luxurious cabin.

Events had moved fast since that decisive moment Bruce found himself lying on the gravel drive. With an effort he'd righted his wheelchair and somehow managed to scramble back into it.

He'd gasped out the story to a startled Alfred, then the detective work began. Bruce had noticed that the SPRANG FLOWERS sign on the kidnappers' van was freshly painted—an obvious ploy to distract attention. But he'd instinctively memorized the license number. It was a rental plate, and he went methodically through "Vehicle Rentals" in the Gotham directory until he found the van's owners.

*Amazing what a dozen phone calls can do!* Alfred marveled as he watched the master at work. The renter—a certain B. Asp—had paid cash but had to leave an address for emergency contact. He was registered at the Ritz Hotel. As a nonresident alien they'd taken his passport details. But Mr. Asp had now checked out, Bruce was told, and yes, now that he asked, a newly painted rental van had been parked in the hotel lot.

Two more calls and he had the name of the cab company whose limo took Asp and his party to the airport. Branson Airways confirmed that a charter plane rented to a Mr. Benedict Asp had taken off an hour earlier. Its destination: London, England.

Alfred had wanted to call in the new Batman's assistance, but Bruce insisted they handle this themselves. "Paul has Gotham to take care of," he'd argued. "He doesn't have time to go abroad."

The plane roared down the runway and soared into the evening air.

*Thwap! Thwump!* Robin's knuckles dug deep into the old sandbag he'd set up in his father's cellar. He paused, wiping sweat from his brow. Somehow working out didn't make him feel any better. There was nothing he could do about his father's disappearance except trust in Bruce.

Robin bit his lip. Bruce had taught him pride is a vice best avoided by someone who wanted to be a hero. He'd apologize, make one final attempt to heal the rift between him and Paul. Apart from anything else, Bruce had left him responsible for Paul. Robin knew he had to be close to the man so he could keep an eye on him.

*What does it matter who makes the first move?* he asked himself as he went down into the tunnel again. *As long as we stop this stupid feud.*

There was a dry, dusty smell, a feeling of recent activity. Suspicious, Robin flicked on his pencil-beam flash.

Stretched across the full width of the access tunnel, rising from floor to ceiling, was a newly built solid brick wall. Paul meant what he said. Their team was through.

"You've cut your last drug deal!"
The brothers Big Mike and Johnny Mahoon almost leapt in the air with shock. Facing them, stepping out of the shadows of the warehouse they used for their evil trade, was a grotesque figure. Dressed in a long black swirling topcoat and a battered stovepipe hat, a scarf muffling his face so only his coal-black eyes could be seen, he might have been mistaken for an undertaker—if it hadn't been for the oversized pistols he held in either hand.

"I'm a debt collector," the Tally Man informed them. "You killed a guy called Buto. His father hired me to pay back the debt."

Big Mike started to bluster an explanation, but the Tally Man wasn't listening. He had been paid his fee and he would collect the debt, no argument. His finger tightened on the trigger.

Batman swung through the city, deep in thought. *Did Bruce ever feel like this?* he wondered. *As if his hatred for injustice, his rage against oppression, were going to burst out of him in an explosion he couldn't hope to control?*

*Probably not,* he realized. Wayne knew his own strengths—his abilities—his limits. But Jean Paul

Valley knew nothing about himself; every time he thought he'd hit the solid ground of his being, the System revealed something new.

The sound of gunshots snapped him from his trance. "That came from the Mahoon warehouse!"

Seconds later Batman was standing over the brothers' bodies, a bag of drugs scattered around them.

He caught a glimpse of flying coattails. The killer was on the fire escape, heading for the roof.

Batman followed. Cautiously he raised his head over the parapet. *Air-con units, aerials, maintenance shed.* Keeping low, presenting as small a target as possible, he rolled onto the roof . . .

And was met by a hail of bullets. The first shots took him in the chest, ricocheting off his lightweight Kevlar body armor. But their impact sent him careening back. As he flailed to keep his balance, he felt fiery streaks where bullets creased his shoulder and his thigh.

Batman lost it, and went plunging down, sixty feet to the ground.

Then it seemed as if his mind exploded, calculating velocity, momentum, and angle of descent. His arm lashed out, seemingly of its own volition, and his tungsten spikes drove a full inch into the building wall. There was a horrendous tearing screech and his arm felt like it had been yanked out of its socket—but he was safe, clinging thirty feet up.

The Tally Man opened up from above with another series of shots. Batman knew sooner or later he'd be hit again. Swinging desperately until his body picked up enough speed, he soared to catch a flagpole, then dropped the remaining distance to the ground.

Up on the roof, the Tally Man fumed. He knew that if he didn't take care of Batman, the Dark Knight would pursue him until he was caught.

The Tally Man leapt from the roof, the specially cut slits in his voluminous coat funneling the updraft, bearing him to the ground. He reloaded as he landed, firing again as he heard something move in the shadows.

But it was a stone Batman had tossed as a diversion, and he dived from hiding while the Tally Man was off-balance. The guns went flying from his grip, but he twisted his body as they fell so that he came out on top.

The Tally Man's fists cracked into Batman's face. "Nothing personal," he rasped. "Just a man doing his job!"

There was a red mist in front of Batman's eyes. When the pain cleared, there was a vision of his father in his head. "On your feet, boy!" The words rolled around his mind. "You are Azrael, Angel of Vengeance! You were made to kill—not to die!"

As suddenly as it appeared, the vision was gone. Batman heaved the Tally Man off as new energy, somehow supplied by the System, surged through him. Then he was on top, the anger still growing as his terrible spikes rose and fell. . . .

A block away and a hundred feet higher, a burly figure watched through binoculars. *This new Batman is impressive,* Bane thought. *Unlike his predecessor, he is willing to spill blood. Good. That will make his ultimate defeat that much more interesting.*

But not tonight. Tonight Bane felt weak. He had to replenish his stock of Venom.

Soon.

"My God! Call an ambulance, Montoya!"

The two police officers stood looking down at the unconscious body of the Tally Man. His clothing was shredded—and in the center of his chest, a large Bat-symbol had been carved in his flesh.

Harvey Bullock sighed. Just as they'd arrived, they'd seen a caped figure make off into the night. "Looks like Gotham's resident vigilante is starting to play rough!"

# Three

London, England. The chimes of Big Ben rang out as the drab gray day shaded into the drab gray night.

A slight mist rose from the sluggish River Thames, seeping up to envelop the riverside buildings of the Houses of Parliament, muffling all sound, giving the old city a strange, otherwordly feel.

A few miles downstream, the tall piers of Tower Bridge rose dizzyingly. On a dockside street on the south bank, derelict for decades, a hunched figure waited.

Sir Hemingford Gray was actually tall and well built, but his body was twisted slightly—the result of a confrontation with a rhino on an African safari, or so the story went. A monocle was clamped in one eye, a bristling mustache covered his top lip, and he leaned heavily on a silver-capped walking cane.

Looking up at the bridge, past the thick suspension cables, Sir Hemingford could see a tiny figure perched right on top. The vigilante known as Hood was taking no chances on an ambush. The modern equivalent of the old English hero Robin Hood, who stole from the rich to give to the poor, he had many enemies.

When Hood was sure it was safe, he leapt. The loose flaps of material that hung between the arms and body of his tight red and white costume caught the air and billowed, a cross between a parachute and wings. He glided expertly down in swift, tight circles to the ground.

"You did what I asked you?" Sir Hemingford asked. In answer, the young English vigilante held up a slim plastic folder. It was stamped TOP SECRET.

"Here's the payment we agreed," the older man went on, taking an envelope from the pocket of his tweed jacket. "The name, date, and exact arrival time of a ship ferrying illegal arms into London from Gotham."

A block away, a Rolls Royce waited. Sir Hemingford winced as he eased himself carefully into the backseat and it headed off.

"Well, Sir Hemingford . . . or is it safe to call

you Master Bruce now?" the driver asked. "Did Hood succeed?"

"He did indeed . . . Alfred."

Under the monocle, the cheek pads that fattened his face, and the fake grizzled mustache, was none other than Bruce Wayne. Master of Disguise had been one of his many talents as Batman; it hadn't deserted him. He was able to walk with a cane now, painfully but for short periods at least, a direct result of Dr. Kinsolving's techniques.

Though his career as a costumed crime fighter was over, Bruce was taking no chances. The playboy fop image of himself he'd so carefully nurtured would never engage in this type of thing; besides, if he was caught as Wayne it would lead straight back to Gotham, perhaps compromising the safety of Tim and Paul. Hence the elaborate disguise.

Bruce opened the plastic folder and pulled out a single sheet. He'd attempted a computer trace on Benedict Asp, which had run into a dead end: all files on the man had been pulled by MI5, the British secret service. But Bruce had a way around that. As Batman he'd kept extensive records on vigilante activity around the world. It had been no trouble to find an English hero willing to put his all on the line in the name of justice and a captured cargo of arms.

Now, Bruce allowed himself a small smile. This

document was exactly what he wanted—the MI5 report on Asp.

It was midafternoon in the Batcave, but Paul couldn't sleep. His head felt light, strange. When he thought about how he'd hurt the Tally Man last night, he felt sick.

"Azrael! My Avenging Angel!"

A large gleaming skull dressed in a medieval chain mail helmet seemed to shimmer hazily in midair. Paul rubbed his eyes incredulously, but it was still there.

It spoke again, the words burning directly into his brain. It was an aspect of St. Dumas, it told him, a little-known fourteenth-century saint.

"I created the first Azrael, to police the order that assumed my name. You should have followed in your father's footsteps. But Fate has decreed differently. You are the Batman. It is your crusade to clean up Gotham. I, Dumas, give you my sanction. You must prepare to fight the worst of evils!"

Then the vision was gone and Paul was left wondering if he'd imagined the whole thing, or if he'd really had a supernatural experience . . . or if it was something implanted by the System for reasons he didn't understand.

"The worst of evils . . ." That could only mean

Bane. Despite what he'd promised Bruce, he vowed to himself now he would be ready.

Automatically, as if it didn't belong to him, his hand picked up a pencil and began to sketch on a sheet of paper.

When he looked down, he'd drawn a design for a completely different Batman costume.

An absurd figure lurched toward the Metro Hotel. His face was covered in a hood with buttons for eyes and a slit for a mouth. Straw protruded from the ankles and wrists of his costume. For all the world he looked like a walking scarecrow.

One minute later the figure detonated a compressed gas cylinder in the busy reception area. Thick, oily Fear Gas began to spread along the corridors.

The reception clerk was the first to breathe it in. His eyes at once took on a terrified, hunted look, and he began to sweat profusely. "Please don't let the termites get me!" he beseeched, swiping at empty air.

Seconds later a fat woman started to scream. "Keep back! You all want to eat me!"

She hit her anxious husband with her bag. As he too breathed the gas, the worst fears in his mind, the ones he'd always kept locked away, came bubbling to the surface.

• • •

On patrol in the Batmobile, Batman heard the reports as he monitored the police wave band.

"Scarecrow at Adelphi Theater—dozens trampled!"

"Gotham Medical Ball—major fire, hundreds injured. Scarecrow apprehended!"

"Fifty-seventh Precinct—officers down! Scarecrow killed!"

Fake Scarecrows, of course. Doubles the real Scarecrow had ensnared with his Fear Gas and forced to do his bidding. Batman recalled the villain's data file from memory: once Dr. Jonathan Crane, a brilliant psychiatrist, he'd been the butt of jokes from his students and colleagues because of his gawky, unkempt appearance. Driven into insanity, he now delighted in causing fear and pain in others.

Another Arkham Asylum escapee—a reminder of why Batman needed to go after Bane.

A huge hologram image of the Scarecrow, several hundred feet high, suddenly lit up the sky over the city center. "Hear me, people of Gotham," a much-magnified voice thundered. "For too long you've laughed at me, treated me with disdain. But no more!"

The words seemed to echo everywhere. He must

have dozens of speakers in position, Batman realized.

"Tonight, Gotham City will fall on its knees and worship me! You will scream praises to the new God of Fear!"

*The man has gone completely over the edge!* Batman hurriedly flicked on the Batmobile's electronic tracking gear. If he could get a triangulation on the image from three separate locations, he could pinpoint exactly where it was coming from.

"There are gods for everything, you see. Gods of war and healing, mountains and money, fireplaces and apple trees. But never before has there been a God of Fear!"

On the rooftop balcony garden of Herold's Antiquarian Books, the real Scarecrow was holding a one-sided conversation with the young student who sat expressionlessly beside him. He had advertized at the university for volunteers for a harmless experiment. They thought they were going to be paid fifty bucks—and instead he'd turned them into zombies.

Now their handiwork could be seen: several buildings were in flames, the flickering light and dark smoke blotting out the stars. *"Hraaaaa! Hrooooo!"* Scarecrow's unearthly laugh rang out across the rooftops.

It was a complete coincidence that one of the

students was Phil Herold, son of the very first man Jonathan Crane had murdered more than a decade ago. He'd decided to keep Phil around, if only out of historical interest. Phil, first terrified and then hypnotized by the crazy Crane, had no option but to sit and listen.

"Tonight we'll change all that, Phil," Scarecrow was saying. "Tonight, I shall become a god!"

Two stories above, a caped figure crouched stock-still, listening to Scarecrow's rant. *He's crazy,* the vigilante called Anarky thought, *a complete fruit-cake!* Lost in his loose-fitting red cape and wide-brimmed hat, Anarky wore a theatrical mask that made it impossible to discern his age. Many a villain who tangled with him, and took a jolt from his powerful taser, would have been astounded to discover the "man" who beat them was only fifteen years old.

A vigilante with a social conscience, Anarky usually went after targets like polluters and corrupt politicians. Scarecrow was way out of his league—a major villain—but now that his skill with electronics had tracked the criminal down, Anarky felt he had to follow through himself.

Suddenly a dark shape went hurtling past him from above, swinging toward the bookshop roof. Batman!

The Scarecrow was taken completely by surprise. Batman slammed into him, the two of them rolling to the ground. His fists rained blows on the ridiculous straw-padded man. Scarecrow kept himself in good physical condition, but he was no match for Batman in a close-quarters fight. His hand dragged a small skull-shaped container from his belt.

When squeezed, the plastic skull gave off a whiff of thick, oily gas that hit Batman in the face. He coughed and fell back as the Fear Gas took immediate effect.

Terror seized him, a horrific fear a hundred times worse than anything he'd ever felt in his whole life. Cold shivers ran up and down his spine, and perspiration beaded his forehead under the cowl. His heart raced. He knew what he was really afraid of—

Not knowing himself. Being a man who had been molded by somebody else. Having the System instead of free will. He was afraid he wasn't a person at all, but some kind of flesh-and-blood robot!

"*Hraaa! Hrooo!*" The Scarecrow was bent double with raucous laughter. "This is even better than I'd hoped for—Gotham's God, and slayer of the Batman, too!"

Then Anarky swooped down. Dangling on his line, he swung over the two men's heads, tossing the folded net he always carried. But Scarecrow saw it at the last moment and dodged clumsily aside. As Anarky landed, Scarecrow raised his arm and sent a metal-tipped straw shooting through the air. The straw hit the vigilante's cloak, and almost immediately he crumpled to his knees.

"Knockout potion," Scarecrow trumpeted. "Nighty-night!"

Batman used the distraction to good effect. His razor claws scythed through Anarky's net and he stepped free. Scarecrow had only one final weapon.

"Phil!" the villain yelled to the mesmerized student. "Throw yourself off the roof!"

The boy got to his feet, eyes blank and zomboid, and shuffled toward the roof edge.

"What are you waiting for, noble Dark Knight?" Scarecrow taunted. "Save the boy—and let me escape! That's the way you work, isn't it? Always save innocent lives first?"

Phil stood at the edge, staring straight ahead, a drop of fifty feet to the street below. Anarky lay close by—the straw dart still embedded in his cloak. Batman's jaw set grimly, then he hurled himself after the escaping Scarecrow. A perfect dive brought him down and had the madman yelling his surrender.

"You let an innocent boy die," Scarecrow said as Batman led him back. "That's not the Batman I know!"

Just then—

"Help—give me a hand!" It was Anarky, wedged against the wall, holding desperately onto his taut line. Without even straining, Batman helped him haul Phil Herold back onto the roof, Anarky's grapnel closed around the boy's ankle.

"But—how?" Scarecrow gasped.

It was Batman who answered. "Because your dart didn't reach him—it stuck in his cloak. Anarky was playing dead—waiting for another opportunity, no doubt."

Anarky looked at him, his eyes bitter under the mask. "You couldn't have known I'd catch him!" he accused. "If I hadn't, the boy would have died—and it would have been *your* fault!"

Batman glared at the vigilante. "And if I hadn't caught Scarecrow, hundreds—perhaps thousands— might have died. As far as I was concerned, there was no contest!"

Anarky watched as Batman swung down to ground level, carrying Scarecrow. *Something isn't right here,* Anarky thought. *The Batman I know would never have taken a chance with an innocent life, even if Scarecrow had escaped! I wonder what's happened to change him?*

# Four

"**B**enedict Asp was unknown to British Intelli-
gence until he was twenty-five." Bruce was
reading from the file Hood had stolen for him.
"Then he undertook research work for secret exper-
iments on psionic powers."

He saw Alfred's frown and explained: "Telepa-
thy, extrasensory perception—the powers of the
mind."

Bruce read on: "Ten years after that, Asp was
reported as being in close touch with the KGB, also
known to be interested in supranormal abilities. He
returned from Russia a moderately wealthy man and
bought himself the lordship and manor house in the
country village of Monkleigh. Because of rumors
concerning a psionic weapon, the British had been

keeping him under light surveillance. They lost him on a trip to Gotham City.''

Bruce and Alfred were in their guises of Sir Hemingford Gray and his manservant Charles, staying at a five-hundred-year-old picture-postcard inn on Monkleigh Green.

It was a hazy afternoon, the country quiet broken only by the sound of leather on willow as the village youths played cricket out on the green.

From the windows of their adjoining rooms, they had a full view of Monkleigh Hall, perched a few hundred yards away on a wooded hill overlooking the surrounding countryside.

''What I can't understand is why he came all that way to kidnap poor Jack Drake and Shondra.'' Bruce's brow was furrowed. He'd been through this a hundred times and still had no satisfactory answer. ''Obviously not for ransom, as no demands have been received.''

Alfred looked up from the local newspaper he'd been reading. ''Something interesting in the Society columns, sir. 'Grand Hunt Ball—Saturday,''' he read aloud. ''That's tonight. And it's being held in Monkleigh Hall!''

Midway through his twentieth leg lift, Bruce paused and grimaced with effort. ''Then I'd better polish up my dance steps!''

•   •   •

In a bare cell under Monkleigh Hall, Dr. Shondra Kinsolving sat at a rough table, facing a huge mute Russian called Yuri. He held a jagged knife in one hand, poised over his other forearm.

Benedict Asp stood behind her, one hand resting on Jack Drake's shoulder. The upheaval of the journey had been too much for Tim's dad; he'd collapsed with breathing difficulties, and now an oxygen mask was strapped over his mouth.

Asp nodded curtly to Yuri, and slowly, deliberately, the man slashed a deep cut in his own arm.

"Now, Shondra," Asp said quietly. "Heal him."

Shondra winced at the blood running down the expressionless Yuri's arm. "No, Benedict!" she burst out. "I've done it a thousand times already! I won't do it again!"

"That's very foolish, Shondra." She was unnerved by the quiet menace in his voice. Without another word he raised his hand and grasped the tube connecting Jack's mouthpiece to his precious oxygen canister. "I told you what would happen to Mr. Drake if you didn't cooperate. Let's just see how well he breathes without the mask."

"Please—don't hurt him," she begged. Asp knew that threatening her directly would have done no good; but he'd long known Shondra's deep devotion to her patients.

His hand froze. "Then heal Yuri!"

As she placed her hands over Yuri's wound, Shondra silently cursed the day her mother had remarried and Asp became her half brother. She began to concentrate and felt that well-known glow start to spread in her mind. Asp also focused on what she was doing, and did the trick with his mind that he had learned when he was a boy. Somehow it amplified her own power, magnifying it, so that the weak psionic talents became much more powerful when they worked together.

The warm glow spread down her arms and out into her fingers, bathing Yuri's wound in the feeling. Before Asp's eyes the cut healed itself, the tissue sealing itself back together as if by magic.

She remembered how it used to be when they were both young and they used their power for good. Then their parents died in a car crash, and they were adopted by their uncle. He was a cruel man, and he used to beat them mercilessly with his buckled leather belt.

It was to protect Benedict from a particularly brutal beating that Shondra had joined her mind with his and tried to force their stepfather back. But instead, he clutched his heart and went into spasm, dying before their eyes. Shondra was petrified, but Benedict just laughed and said their uncle got what he deserved.

The next day Shondra had packed her few belongings and fled. She changed her name and eventually wound up in Gotham City, where no one had ever heard of her. She put herself through college, became a doctor, and made a decent life for herself . . . until Asp tracked her down.

In the cell next door, ex–Colonel Vega of the KGB's elite Paranormal Unit sat before a bank of sensitive electronic equipment. When Shondra's healing power had been unleashed, he'd been able to harness and store it in the special batteries he'd designed and built. Attached to these prototype batteries was a small device, a cross between stereo headphones and a metal baseball cap.

Asp entered the cell and watched in silence as Vega flicked a dial and the device began to pulse and glow. He held it out toward the cage that stood on the floor.

Invisible psionic rays streamed out, washing over the two large rats that scurried around inside the bars. They paused, whiskers twitching. Then without a sound they dropped down dead.

"Perfect!" Vega said admiringly, flicking off the switch again. "With this we can kill anyone, anywhere, at any distance. There is no defense against it. The governments of the world will pay us millions—billions—for it!"

"The ultimate assassins!" Asp savored the words. "We'll be the most powerful men on earth!"

Monkleigh Hall was bathed in light as dozens of the local great and good arrived for the traditional ball.

"Your invitation, sir?"

"My man has it. He's parking the Rolls," Sir Hemingford Gray said casually, brushing past the security man at the door with arrogant authority.

Bruce was in! He cast his eyes around, taking in the Tudor beams and the ancient tapestries and carvings. No sign of Asp. But he'd have to show sooner or later. He was the host, after all.

"Just one last time, my dear." Asp stood behind Shondra, Vega's psionic helmet clamped lightly to his head. Shondra didn't know it—she didn't know anything about what he was doing—but tonight was the big one. The final test. She sighed and placed her hands over Yuri's bloody arm.

Benedict Asp felt her healing energy come through as he had so often in the past. He felt himself catch it in his mind, using his own natural power to amplify and direct it. Then the little twist— the change of focus that altered everything, that turned good into evil.

Asp thought of the old coaching inn. Many villagers would be there now for the Saturday night dinner special. On the village green the cricket game went on, bathed in the light of two streetlights.

And then Benedict Asp willed them dead.

In the inn, the men at the bar paused; their eyes rolled, and they dropped without a sound. Two women gossiping at the open front door fell together, an instant before the families inside succumbed. A car driver slumped over his wheel; the car mounted the sidewalk, struck a wall, and came to rest, its engine still running. On the green, the cricket game was over forever.

"Benedict, I—I'm going to be sick!" Shondra lurched to her feet, one hand on her stomach. "I need air!"

Asp laid down the helmet, took her arm, and led her to the cell door. "Colonel—Yuri—come. You can bring her back here when I make my appearance at the ball."

They hurried up the stairs that led to the secret exit by the garden pagoda.

Asp opened the door, looked out to check that the coast was clear—and came face-to-face with a startled Sir Hemingford Gray, who'd come outside for a breath of air.

"Shondra!"

Asp pushed Shondra back and slammed the door

before the disguised Bruce could react. Dragging her past Yuri and Colonel Vega, he snapped an order: "Someone's recognized us. Kill him!"

Sir Hemingford threw open the door just as Yuri charged up the stairs. Hemingford stepped smartly back and jammed the cane between the Russian's ankles. Yuri tripped and fell, and before he could get up again the cane hit him sharply behind one ear.

Vega was an intellectual, an inventor—and certainly no fighter. "Please, no violence," he begged, cringing away. But Sir Hemingford couldn't take the chance. He clipped him on the point of the chin.

Asp had dragged the struggling Shondra back to the cell, where he snatched up the psi-helmet. He just had time to put it on his head when the door flew open.

"Shondra—it's me!" Bruce broke off as Asp focused on him and concentrated.

At once there was a pounding in his head, and his legs began to buckle.

Shondra stood rooted to the spot. *Bruce Wayne—here—in disguise?* She didn't know how—but she could see with her own eyes that Asp was killing him. Concern drove her into action.

"Stop it!" She grabbed Asp's arm and started to concentrate, pouring out her healing power.

Asp quivered as the extra psi-power coursed through him. He hadn't expected this! It was too

much. He couldn't control it. He tried to grab the
helmet and dash it from his head—but it was too
late. The amplified power fed back into his mind . . .
and exploded.

Shondra felt nauseated, exhausted. Bruce lay on
the floor, his breathing ragged, a thin trickle of
blood coming from one ear. She knelt beside him.

"You can't die," she whispered. "I won't let
you!" She fought off waves of weakness, closed
her eyes, and summoned the remaining power she
had left.

Bruce felt himself being pulled back as if from
the edge of some bottomless abyss. Groaning, he
opened his eyes. He felt strange—but it wasn't until
he sat up that he realized what the difference was:
his back. There was no pain, no dull throb, no ache.

He almost broke out in a grin—then he saw Asp
lying dead, Jack Drake unconscious but breathing
in his chair . . . and curled up on the floor, Shondra.

Her eyes were blank. She didn't recognize him.
But she clutched at his hand like a child, whimper-
ing softly over and over and over again.

The strain had been too much. Shondra's mind
had broken down completely.

Emotions Bruce hadn't felt since his parents died
welled up inside him. To have come so close . . . but
to have lost her, too! Bruce felt as if he had won a
battle, yet lost the war.

# Five

**B**atman swooped through the Gotham night like some monstrous bird of prey. The new costume, born of Jean Paul Valley's fevered trance, made him far more dangerous, more sinister, than ever before.

The new cape grabbed the wind and swelled on its lift. He was a dark angel on jagged wings.

*Truly this is the role I have been born for,* he thought to himself. His fear of the System was forgotten. The hands that had shaped him had done their job well. *I will the best Batman there could ever be.*

Somewhere out there in the wild city, Bane was at large. Tonight, no matter what, there would be a showdown.

•   •   •

Two hundred yards behind him Robin followed, moving more cautiously than he ever had before. Batman's new costume looked lethal. He knew he'd be in real trouble if his presence were spotted.

Maybe it was something in the air—or some unfathomed bond between them—but Bane, too, knew tonight was the night. He would confront the upstart, the impostor, and choke the life from him with his bare hands.

He was in Gotham Square, looking up at the flashing neon madness.

And he knew exactly how to find his man.

Batman dropped toward the city center. Out of the corner of his eye he saw the giant neon billboard go dark, only to light up again a moment later.

B–A–T . . . the letters flashed. It could only be Bane! . . . M–A–N H–E–R–E N–O–W.

Batman pulled in his cape and fell faster. He was ready!

In his office at the police department, Commissioner Gordon sat at his desk by the window.

He had a good view of Gotham Square and had often cursed that great billboard as it winked its various messages on and off, night after night. When he saw what it said now he did a double take and snatched up the phone. "Bullock? All available units to Gotham Square! I think there's going to be trouble!"

The trouble had already started.

Just as Batman landed on the narrow ledge in front of the sign, nearly thirty feet above the ground, there was an almighty crash, and Bane came diving straight through it. "Impostor!" he was yelling. "Tonight I reveal you for the fake you are!"

Lightbulbs popped and bare wires sparked. Batman felt as if he'd been hit by a train.

Locked together, they plunged off the roof and down, landing on top of a parked car and demolishing it.

Neither man was even winded. "I'm no fake!" Batman snarled. "I'm the real thing—as you're about to learn!"

Batman's feet came up, straightened, and sent Bane's body flying off, to collide with a large plastic garbage bin at the corner of the square. There was a squeal of brakes as a car swerved to avoid the rolling bin, then a crash as the cab behind piled into it.

Bane rolled to his feet, as fast as anyone Batman had ever faced. He had to stop this man—by any means. His arm came up and he triggered the compressed-air mechanism that fired the shurikens from his glove. Three of the bat-shaped, razor-sharp discs spun through the air in formation.

At the last moment Bane raised his arm, the three blades gouging deep into it. Batman was already leaping forward into a handspring, his feet lashing Bane in the face. He followed through as Bane staggered back, spiked fists lashing out cruelly time after time.

"Curse you!" Bane gritted his teeth as pain coursed through him. This wasn't how it was supposed to be! He had underestimated his foe—this new Batman was strong and smart and knew his moves cold.

Traffic all around had come to a complete stand-still as drivers deserted their vehicles to get a view of the fight. Several police cars were caught in the gridlock, sirens whooping in vain to clear a path. Tight-lipped, Gordon quickly led his men on foot.

Bane had the Dark Knight, one hand clutching his throat in an iron grip, the other clenched and pulled back for another blow. Batman choked, managing to gasp out the word "Light!"—and the voice-activated flare concealed in his chest-plate burst into blinding life.

While Bane cursed and clutched at his eyes, Batman tripped him, punching him twice on the way down. Bane grunted as he came down on the road, his hand fumbling with the stud on his glove.

"More Venom," Bane hissed. Even as he felt the power surge, Batman attacked again. The talons on his gloves raked out, severing the tubes connected to Bane's skull. Liquid gurgled and splashed and spilled.

Bane screamed his rage and unleashed a wild roundhouse kick that caught Batman off-balance and stopped him in his tracks. But Batman was pleased with his handiwork. "I've found your weakness," he said softly. "Your dependence on Venom! Without your drug, you're just another muscular thug!"

Bane took to his heels and ran. He had to get away, find time to think—repair his shattered drug supply. Batman ran after him. The fight wasn't over, but he had no doubt now that he would win. Eventually.

Bane ran around one of the support pillars on which the elevated railroad track ran. Grabbing the girders, he swung himself up the ten feet onto the track. A train stood at the station above, its doors already sliding closed as it prepared to pull out. Bane hurled himself inside.

Only a few seconds behind, Batman arrived too late. Without stopping to think, he dug his claws into the outside of a train car and was yanked off his feet.

Bane ran through the train's cars toward the engine, shouldering late-night travelers roughly aside. He ripped open the door to the driver's cabin. One look at the size of Bane was enough; the driver fled back into the train. Meanwhile, Bane grasped the accelerator handle and jammed it up to full speed. The farther he could get from Batman—and the faster—the better.

Suddenly, shattering glass showered him as the cab window splintered open and Batman came swinging in, feetfirst.

Swinging between two Gothic buildings, Robin tried to keep the train in sight. This whole thing was an unmitigated disaster! He didn't know what he could do to stop it—he'd be shredded like paper if he tried to step in between these two.

The train was going faster, rattling around a wide curve. Desperately, the boy raced across the rooftops, trying to cut it off and get slightly ahead.

On board, people were screaming as the cars clattered about on the rails, tossing them around. But the two men in the driver's cab were engaged in all-out war and paid no attention to what was going on around them.

Robin leapt onto a low bridge and timed it just

right, dropping onto the speeding train as it shot underneath. Legs bent, he landed just one carriage behind the engine.

He pulled a small metal canister from his belt. Fighting to keep his balance on the wildly swaying roof, he paused to look ahead. The train was coming up to a wide bend—at this speed they'd never take it! He tossed the canister down into the space between the engine and the car. A second later, there was a small but powerful explosion, and the couplings parted.

The rear cars immediately began to slow—but the engine, relieved of its load, shot ahead with renewed vigor, roaring toward the curve at sixty-plus.

Batman and Bane were thrown around like rag dolls as the engine-car failed to make the bend. It leapt the tracks with a horrific rending of metal. The car hung in the air for a moment, then fell, smashing through the walls of a derelict shopping block.

It was a full minute before Robin came upon the wreck. There was debris everywhere, and the air was full of thick, choking dust. His heart leapt to his mouth as a burly shape came toward him. Bane?

No. The figure was tired, aching, and bloodied . . . but it was Batman who stood triumphant. He walked from the disaster, dragging the semiconscious Bane behind him.

"Finish me," Bane panted. "There's nothing for me now. Kill me!"

For a moment it looked as if Batman would grant his wish. His razor claws were poised to strike.

Robin froze. Would Paul do it? Would he take that final, irretrievable step that would brand him a murderer, no better than the criminals he sought to stop? *Was* he the Batman . . . or was he Azrael, the programmed Angel of Vengeance and Death?

Batman lowered his hand and stepped back.

"No. You're broken, Bane. Blackgate Prison can hold the pieces."

Robin almost cheered. For a moment, he'd been afraid Paul would kill Bane, then turn on Robin himself for following him.

Batman put a hand on the teenager's shoulder, resting it there lightly. A small gesture—but Robin knew that it meant their feud was over.

"I have to admit, I still don't like the way you do things," Robin said. "But there's no denying, they *do* get done! I was wrong about you. You've earned the right to wear the costume—new or old. You *are* the Batman!"

For the first time in many nights, two figures moved through Gotham City's rooftops together.

# PART III

# KNIGHTSEND

# One

**A**ll went well . . . for a while.
    During the day, Paul lived in the Batcave, working out, sleeping, devising weapons for his fearsome new costume. And if he continued to see his visions, they didn't seem to trouble him now.

At night he took care of business the way Batman always did. Villains of the caliber of the Ventriloquist and Scarface, Dr. Faustus, and Firefly were all locked up in Blackgate Prison, awaiting the rebuilding of Arkham Asylum.

But there was one inmate he hadn't caught who was causing him a lot of frustration: Abattoir, a serial killer who only went after members of his own family. So far twenty-five of his relations, from parents to second cousins, had been murdered. Now he had only one relative surviving in the Gotham area, his cousin, Graham Etchison. After he was taken care of, Abattoir intended to move to California and pursue his family's western branch.

Cold eyes watched as Batman swung toward Gotham Cathedral, just across the street from Etchison's apartment, and landed on a high ledge. He looked quite at home on the roof of the hundred-year-old building, a bat-monster among the grotesque stone gargoyles.

The hairs on the back of his neck stiffened. Someone was watching him. But who—and where?

As if in answer, one of the large stone beasts began to slowly detach itself from the wall.

A block away, on the deserted late-night street, plainclothes officers Dugan and Rayner were fed up. They'd pulled surveillance on Etchison every night this week, sitting hours in their car waiting for a killer who never showed.

"Think that could be him?" Dugan nodded toward a man wrapped in an old raincoat, shambling along the street toward them. The guy's hat brim was pulled down over his eyes, and what little could be seen of his face seemed dark and shiny. "Better check him out."

Dugan opened the door and got out, his hand slipping his nightstick from his belt.

The man in the raincoat suddenly pulled off one of the thick gloves that he wore. His hand brushed away the nightstick as if it were a toothpick, then clamped on the policeman's face.

The hand was made of thick, pliant mud . . . and it burned.

Rayner recognized Preston Payne—alias Clayface—one of Gotham's most dangerous criminals. The officer drew his gun and fired off several shots as Clayface let Dugan crumple to the sidewalk. But that oozing, ugly mud-flesh burned so much the bullets melted before they even got to their target.

Preston Payne had been a top scientist until his fateful decision to self-test a new blood serum he'd discovered. Instead of gaining the plasticity of shape he sought, allowing him to change his form to anything he desired, the serum became a fiery cancer burning inside his altered flesh.

He was in almost constant pain. And the only way to relieve it was to pass on his contagion by burning someone else to death.

Once again his awful hand reached out, and Detective Rayner screamed.

The grotesque gargoylelike beast cannoned into Batman, sweeping him from his perch. But before he fell from the ledge, he managed to grab onto its legs. The beast's heavy stone wings flapped frantically, holding them hovering in the air.

Batman knew at once who his foe was. He'd studied the Batcave files until he knew every villain Bruce Wayne had ever faced. This could only be Lady Clayface.

Blessed—or cursed—with the shape-changing power her partner Clayface had so desperately sought, she was able to assume the strength and abilities of whatever she mimicked.

Dangling from her stone claws, the ground a long, dizzying way below, Batman did the unexpected. He swung his body, kicking up forcefully, slamming his feet into her beak. Before she could recover he'd shifted position and grabbed a wing.

"Let go!" she shrieked. "I can't hold us both!"

But Batman clung on, and they spiraled down through the branches of a tree to land on the grass below.

Lady Clayface was changing already, her seemingly solid stone body now melting and flowing, reforming itself into a new shape. Thick tubular coils of clay wrapped around Batman's body, enfolding him the way a boa constrictor seizes its prey, threatening to crush him.

"You're different from before, Batman!" Lady Clayface's head had formed atop the serpentlike body. "But you'll die just the same!"

The coils closed tighter, trapping his arms at his sides. Only his head and shoulders were visible as he fought for freedom. Just then Preston Payne came shuffling over.

"Don't kill him!" His voice oozed rather than spoke. "I want that pleasure myself!"

Batman felt the heat as a sticky clay hand reached out for his face. He struggled, but the coils held him fast.

"Flame!" he gasped.

The voice-activated flamethrower he'd built into the costume's left arm flared, its searing heat trapped by Lady Clayface's coils. Batman suffered too, though the insulating layers in his costume saved him from the worst of it. Lady Clayface's grip slackened as she cursed with pain, and Batman wriggled free. He rolled forward, knocking Clayface over.

The creature tottered and fell, thrashing blindly for something to hold onto.

Instead, he found his partner's coils. She writhed in a frenzy as his hand touched her.

Batman left Payne squatting beside Lady Clayface, garbling apologies, and ran across the street. Quickly he climbed the stairs to Graham Etchison's apartment. He'd heard the police sirens coming closer and knew a specialist team from the authorities would take care of the clay couple.

One solid boot sent Etchison's door off its hinges.

Inside, stooping over his cringing victim, Abattoir cursed. It had cost him every cent he had to pay the Clayfaces to act as decoys, and they'd failed him. Whipping out a pistol, Abattoir squeezed off five shots in quick succession. He watched in dismay as they ricocheted from Batman's Kevlar-lined costume.

"Only one bullet left, Abattoir."

"Yeah." He swiveled and pointed the gun at his cousin's head. "So come any closer an' Cousin Graham gets it!"

Graham Etchison was a mild, ineffectual man. He was scared witless by what was going on.

"No tricks! I mean it!" Abattoir roughly hauled his cousin to his feet and started to back out through the small kitchen to the French windows that gave onto the outside fire escape.

"Put the gun down." Batman stalked purposefully after them.

Abattoir's finger tightened on the trigger. "Keep back or I kill him!"

Still Batman came on.

From the shadows of a rooftop directly across the street, Robin watched in horror as the tragedy unfolded.

•    •    •

Abattoir's back was against the fire escape rail. Batman took one more step. Then there was a sharp "pop" as the gun went off, and Graham Etchison fell dead.

Batman ducked as Abattoir threw the gun. Then Batman pivoted on one foot and raised the other in a spectacular karate kick that sent the serial killer back against the rusty railing. It gave with a shriek of metal, and Abattoir plunged to his death.

Robin knew he had to have it out with Batman this time. This was serious! Two men dead—and no question that both deaths were Batman's fault.

But if the boy had expected regret—contrition—concern—he was to be sadly disappointed.

The sneer was evident in Paul's voice. "Abattoir deserved to die," he stated baldly. "Etchison's death was a pity . . . but if it meant a stop to Abattoir's murderous campaign, it was worth it!"

Robin didn't argue. He could see there was no point; he'd never be able to convince this arrogant, swaggering man he had once called his friend. Whatever had happened to Paul, it had taken him past the point of no return.

The next day, Tim Drake rose and readied himself for school. His dad was home now, though

Bruce and Alfred had sent a card to say they were staying on in England for a vacation. Tim had hired a bustling Irish housekeeper, Mrs. McIlvaine, to look after his father. Jack seemed to be responding well to her brisk no-nonsense ways, and her cheery "auld country" brogue lifted his spirits.

When the phone rang halfway through breakfast, Tim answered.

"Top floor apartment, One Delano Street, seven tonight. Be there." Tim didn't recognize the voice, but the next words sent a shiver down his spine. "I know your secret identity."

Long before the appointed hour that night, Robin was crouched behind a rooftop parapet fifty yards from the apartment. *Information is power,* he was thinking. *This guy knows about me; I should know who he is before I go in to face him.*

The Boy Wonder racked his brain trying to figure who it could be. He'd always been careful to cover his tracks, never leaving behind any personal clues. No one at school could remotely suspect—why, even his dad, who lived in the same house, didn't know about his son's double life. He had plenty of enemies, of course—but how would they have found out?

A slow grin broke over his face as realization dawned. *Of course! Who else could it be?*

"Bruce! You're looking great!"

And indeed Bruce *was* looking great. He'd put on weight, was walking without the cane, and was now completely healed by the sacrifice Shondra had made. The apartment was one of several he owned throughout the city, in case he ever had to hide out for cover.

"I'm sorry for the subterfuge, Robin," he apologized, "but I didn't want any fuss. Besides, figuring out my identity was a nice test of your abilities!" His face grew serious as he went on: "I've decided to dedicate to charity work the energy I previously gave to crime fighting. I won't be around much in future."

Alfred was there, too, pleased at the reunion. But Robin only half-listened as they told of their adventures in England. He wanted to tell his own story—about Paul.

Robin felt confused; he needed advice from older, wiser shoulders. Bruce had been his mentor, his partner, his friend—but now Bruce had his own life to run, and he'd moved on from crime fighting. Robin didn't want to burden him with things that no longer concerned him.

"Tim?" He realized Bruce was saying his name. "Is something wrong?"

"No," he said quickly, then thought the better of it. Bruce was his friend; the very least he deserved was honesty. "Yes," he corrected himself. "Something is very, very wrong!"

# Two

The sun was rising, and day was no time for the Bat.

Jean Paul figured he'd spend the day in the Bat-cave, working on the new costume developments he'd devised. A voice-activated laser would come in handy, and he wanted to look into the possibility of connecting his visor via microwave to the computers.

He strode from the parking bay—and found Bruce Wayne seated calmly on a spur of rock, waiting.

If Paul was surprised, he didn't show it. "How did you get in?" His tone was almost offhand. "I thought I'd blocked up all entrances."

"I've had more than twenty years to learn the secrets of these caverns," Bruce told him. "You've broken the code of the Batman, Paul. I vowed never to kill. No man has the right to take the life of another. And though I didn't do it, you wore the costume that I gave you. You killed Abattoir in *my* name!''

Bruce wished Paul would take off the cowl so he could see past the filters and into his eyes. But Paul didn't.

''I'm asking you man to man,'' Bruce continued. ''Take the costume off now. Turn your back on all this—before you lose control and kill again.''

Batman loomed over Bruce, the costume and cape making him appear large and omnipotent while Bruce in slacks and casual jacket felt unprotected and vulnerable.

He saw the blow coming but had no chance to avoid it, Paul moved so fast. But it wasn't a punch, merely a sharp slap that stung his cheek and set his ears ringing.

''You're washed up, old man,'' Paul snapped. ''Finished!'' He slapped him again, a contemptuous backhand that knocked Bruce against the wall. ''The costume, the Cave—they're not yours anymore!'' Again a savage slap. ''They're mine! I'm Batman now! And I'll never give it up!''

His face stinging, but more humiliated than hurt, Bruce faded back into the shadows.

''That's right! Run!'' The words followed him as he squirmed through a gap in the rock only he knew about. "I'll *really* hurt you if you ever show your face here again!"

As Bruce made his way along dark passages to emerge on the hillside below the manor, he cursed himself for the fool he was. He realized only too well now that what Robin had said was true—he'd made a mistake appointing his successor. Jean Paul Valley was on the point of exploding. When someone as powerful as he is cannot control that power, then for the sake of innocent people everywhere, he has to be stopped.

*No man has the right to take another's life,* Bruce thought. *That's why I spent all those years training, so I would never have to use a gun, would never have to kill. And for a killer to wear the mantle of the Bat . . . it makes me feel sick to my gut!*

Whatever had caused Paul's downfall—the awesome responsibility, the constant danger and stress, the unknown effects of the System—the mistake had been Bruce's. And Bruce knew it was up to him to fix it.

In the feeble light of their room's only bare bulb, three cheerless hoodlums glared at the TV screen, which was at that moment showing their pictures.

"—Bane's associates remain at large," the news

announcer was saying. "Police suspect they have escaped with millions of illegal dollars!"

Bird cursed and threw an empty beer can that bounced off the set. "We have nothing! Not a bean!"

After the defeat and arrest of the trio's boss, the police immediately sent SWAT teams into their hotel suite. They were lucky enough to escape with their skins. Since then, the three had been holed up here, back in the dingy Bates Hotel.

Police were watching all routes out of the city. Without Bane to do their thinking and planning, the fugitives were reduced to what they really were: three rather ordinary thugs who maybe knew how to train a hawk or throw a knife, but knew nothing of what it took to become criminal masterminds.

Batman crouched noiselessly on the hotel roof. It had taken him a long time to find them, requiring a lot of the detective work he loathed so much. Hours of threatening small-time snitches, checking seedy bars and dockside flophouses. But at last . . .

He attached his line to the base of a flagpole. Holding tight to the other end, he stepped off the edge of the roof and swung down. Fifteen feet below, his momentum and angle of swing took him crashing feetfirst through the amazed gang's room window.

Bird was the first to recover his wits. "Last time he beat us, it was one on one," he snarled. "Maybe he's changed the costume—but he still can't take all three of us at once!"

But Batman could. And he did. Easily.

Nightwing paused by the water tower and checked behind him. No one. Good. Not that he'd expected to be followed, but it was always better to be safe rather than sorry.

He'd been in Seattle, putting the finishing touches to a case he'd been working on, when the call came. He listened quietly to the caller, then headed directly for the airport and a flight to Gotham City.

He tapped on the door of the Delano Street apartment and a moment later was inside, warmly shaking hands with his old mentor, Bruce Wayne.

"I need your help," Bruce told him. Before he heard another word, Nightwing said, "You have it."

Quickly Bruce related the whole sorry saga of the new Batman and the gratuitous deaths.

Nightwing's lips were tight as he heard of Bruce's personal humiliation; his offer was spontaneous and genuine. "Just tell me where to find him—I'll take the Bat-suit back, all right!"

Bruce shook his head. "You're good, Nightwing—nobody knows that better than I do. But Paul's on another level. He's aided by his System, and he's turned my costume into a weapon in its own right. What I want is for you to keep tabs on him for a while—with a little help from another friend of mine."

The kitchen door opened and Robin stepped into the room. Nightwing was pleased to see him; he genuinely liked the boy.

Under his mask, Robin's eyes were bright. He hadn't felt this good since . . . since he didn't remember when.

Bruce was still talking: "I'm going to be gone about a month—"

"Gone?" Robin frowned. "You mean, taking up your charity work?"

"That was the plan," Bruce said seriously. "But things have changed. I made Paul into Batman—it's my job to unmake him!"

"But you're in no condition—" Nightwing protested.

"Exactly. And that's why I'll be gone about a month." He smiled, but there was an underlying seriousness to his words. "If all goes well, I'll be coming back as what I was—the Batman!"

"The one *true* Batman," Robin whispered under his breath.

# Three

The Golden Lion of the Orient Temple in Gotham's Chinatown was little more than a renovated loft, completely devoid of furniture except for a small raised platform at one end.

Seated cross-legged on the pile of cushions piled atop the platform was a man with no arms. He nodded slightly as the figure standing before him bowed.

"You are the Master Shao, world's finest exponent of the Barefoot fighting technique." The standing figure wore loose-fitting Chinese-style clothes, a scarf wound around the face. But the voice was a woman's.

The Master nodded again. "Only one woman would have the audacity to come here. You are Lady Shiva—the world's deadliest assassin, as some say.'' Her very presence in this temple was a challenge that honor would not let him deny. Gracefully he shrugged off his robe, exposing the shoulder stubs where his arms had been ripped out long ago by overenthusiastic Red Guards.

Lady Shiva pulled the scarf from her face to reveal the mask she wore, that of a stylized demonic bat.

''I had heard you are as beautiful as you are lethal. I would like to see that beauty before I kill you.''

''In your dreams,'' Shiva snapped. ''The Mask of Tengu stays!''

It lasted no more than a minute, a high-speed exchange of blows. When Shiva walked out, Shao lay dead.

The Master's servant Song Li entered as she left. He shrank away from the ugly bat-mask and cried out when he saw the broken body of his master.

Thirty minutes later, Shiva was back at her villa in the hills to the south of Gotham. Only when she was inside did she drop off the loose clothes to reveal the tight cutaway costume she wore underneath.

The man waiting for her was in full black ninja gear, his face swathed and hidden except for his eyes.

"You came to see me last night," Shiva said, "and told me you were once Batman. I believe you. You asked me to help you become Batman again. I said that I would."

She thrust the mask at him. He took it, puzzled. "You are free to train where you want," she continued, "as long as you always wear the Mask of Tengu. Be alert at all times. You will be tested."

Lady Shiva and Batman had crossed paths many times, but the conclusion had always been unsatisfactory. Her philosophy was always to fight to the death, while his was never to take a life.

This time, though, she thought she had him. Master Shao had three disciples, each expert in a different form of fighting. All three would want to hunt down and destroy their mentor's killer . . . the one who wore the Mask of Tengu!

She had made sure the disciples would find him. Odds were, at least one of them would die. Only then would Batman be ready for her.

The next few days saw Bruce settle into an arduous routine.

He camped out above a ravine at the foot of a sheer rock face with a single lightning-blasted tree growing at the top. He rose before the sun each morning and, obeying Lady Shiva, donned the mask. After an hour's meditation, he warmed up with an hour's run, then set out to climb the high cliff.

The rest of the day was spent in workouts and martial arts exercises: blocking, parrying, thrusting, and pivoting, time and time and time again until his body did it naturally, without thought.

By sundown each night, Bruce was exhausted—yet his day was far from over. His mind also had to be exercised and disciplined; the mental techniques he'd learned in the Orient during his training years stood him in good stead now.

He quickly felt the difference the concentrated regime was making, as his mind sharpened daily and his body returned to the lean, muscular fighter he had once been.

It happened on the seventh morning. He had just scaled the cliff, a task that was becoming easier every day; he no longer arrived at the top raw-lunged and panting.

"Tengu! You have slain my sensei!" a tattooed man accused. He carried a long, thin steel chain in each hand, their ends weighted with steel balls. "You will die at the hands of Chainmaster!"

Without warning, one of the long chains whipped through the air. Bruce dived toward him, away from the cliff edge, under the swing.

*This must be the test Shiva mentioned. Trust her to send a chain-wielding maniac!*

Bruce changed direction, then spun and rolled again as the second chain clanked dangerously close. As he passed the burned tree, his foot lashed out, cracking a low branch. He grabbed it, wrenched it free, and twisted to his feet.

The first chain missed his bat-mask by inches. As the second chain bore down on him, Bruce stuck out the branch with split-second timing. The chain whipped around it, and Bruce pulled with all his might. Chainmaster was yanked toward him, Bruce's head cracking against his chin. The man went out like a light.

He wondered how the man had found him in this remote spot. A thought occurred to him and he removed the Mask of Tengu, examining it closely. A tiny radio transmitter was wedged into a corner of the inside. No doubt Shiva had issued receivers to the disciples—and probably killed the master herself.

He began to crush the miniature bug, then thought the better of it. *Let them come,* he decided. *I need the practice!*

Later that night, Bruce stood on the highest point of Wayne Tower. One hundred-plus stories. Once you took that leap, you had only one chance to come out of it—about a third of the way down and off to the side was the roof of a lower building. The gargoyle on its corner was just within Batline range. If the line caught, he would swing to the apex of his flight, let go, somersault in the air, and reach to grasp a flagpole from which he'd swing onto the statue of Justice atop City Hall. If the line didn't catch, he fell and died.

Bruce remembered the first night—

He was twenty-one years old, and it was the final test he'd set for himself before he went on the streets as Batman.

If he could plunge from the tower and cheat death, he reasoned, he'd be ready to start his one-man crusade against crime. He'd been afraid, but with the recklessness of youth he'd taken the plunge.

But as he looked down now he felt a twinge of doubt, the merest flicker of fear. He wasn't ready.

Not yet.

He spent the next week of mornings in the Gotham River, fifty miles upstream from where it hit the sea. The water was still fresh and clear here, and he dived and swam and shot the rapids on a tree trunk.

Evenings he spent pounding the shoulder of the highway, hardly used now since the new interstate opened.

One night at sunset a tall man launched his attack as Bruce ran under the broad cloverleaf overpass. The man dropped silently from the roadway twenty feet above, landing on Bruce's shoulders and pitching him to the ground.

The man was thin and rangy, well over seven feet tall. His reach was incredible and gave formidable power to his blows. He landed several punishing shots as Bruce tried in vain to get close to him.

Mind racing, turning over all the alternatives, Bruce backed away into the shadows where the highway exit ramp came down to meet the ground. *Of course!*

As the tall man lunged after him, Bruce stooped, allowed himself to be caught, then shuffled backward. He pulled the tall man after him, forcing him to duck to get his head under the concrete ramp.

Then Bruce swung a punch—a driving uppercut. The tall man jerked his head back away from the blow—and smashed it straight into the concrete that was a full foot lower than him. He was out cold for hours.

Bruce was camped up at a long-abandoned lumber camp for the final two weeks, on a broad plateau above the river. He hacked logs and chopped wood until his shoulder and arm muscles bulged.

A massive pile of logs stood at the top of the slope

behind the ramshackle buildings that had somehow withstood the ravages of time. Every hour on the hour he sprinted up the slope and climbed it.

That's where the third attacker struck.

As Bruce cleared the slope and ran toward the log pile, the disciple known as Whiplash used her bullwhip to rip out the rotting wedges that restrained the massive heap.

Pulling up in horror, Bruce saw the pile start to move, slowly at first. Then the first logs thundered down on him and he was fighting for his life. He ducked the first two-ton monster as it went rumbling over his head and as good as tasted the bark on the second. The next log was rolling straight on. Bruce leapt onto it, his mind still now, his body acting of its own volition, the way only a top athlete's does. He leapt again, ducking and dodging, constantly moving to keep his balance in the mountain of wood that rolled and thundered around him.

It seemed to last forever but was over in five or six seconds. As Bruce springboarded off a final log, Whiplash drew back her thong.

It was one of the toughest fights Bruce had ever fought. But his body was lean and hard now, his lungs sound, and his eye true. He took his share of blows but always contrived to be rolling with them, or ducking away. And finally he triumphed.

As Bruce stepped back from his fallen foe, the

last rays of the setting sun picked out the erratic flight of the night's first bat.

An omen . . . ?

"Take back your mask, Shiva. I'm finished with it."

"Then Shao's disciples are dead?"

"Shao's disciples are wounded, but they're very much alive. No doubt you hoped I'd kill one, so we could fight on your terms?" Bruce shrugged. "Sorry, Shiva. I've seen the horror of death close up. I will never knowingly inflict it on another being."

Bruce turned on his heel and strode out, and though Shiva hated being foiled, she couldn't help but respect a man of honor.

Midnight. Bruce stood atop Wayne Tower and walked confidently to the edge. He hefted the Bat-line in his hand, considering it for but one moment. He knew.

He was ready.

Pausing only for one final sweeping glance at the city lights below, he dived headfirst off the edge and plunged down, down, down.

# Four

There were twelve men in the warehouse storing stolen army weapons, but Batman charged in headlong, seeming to revel in the thrill of danger as he was met by a hail of lead.

The costume was virtually bulletproof now, and his flamethrower, laser, and shurikens soon silenced the chattering guns. Two or three of the criminals had escaped through the rear door during the fight, now too long gone for him to catch up. But his keen eye saw something on the ground outside that he stooped to pick up.

It was an ancient silver medallion, enscribed on one side with the image of St. Dumas, and on the other with the sigils and symbols of the order that followed him. A shiver ran down Batman's spine. He knew this coin!

His father had carried it all his life, given it by his father before him, back through the centuries. He'd never have relinquished that medal voluntarily; it had been taken from him. His father had said a name before he died—LeHah. Of all the villains he had crushed, LeHah was the one he wanted most.

"You!" Batman grabbed one of the thugs he'd wounded and hauled him roughly to his feet. "Tell me where I find LeHah!"

The man groaned in pain. "I—I don't know. I swear!"

Batman thrust him aside. Someone in Gotham knew. One way or the other, Batman would find out.

"What was that all about, Nightwing?" Robin asked, and his companion shrugged.

They'd been following the Dark Knight as per Bruce's instructions. Batman was becoming even more violent, using brutality as a weapon. Neither hero had much sympathy for criminals, but basic common decency said you didn't hit anyone at all unless you absolutely had to.

"He's moving off," Nightwing observed. "Come on. We'd better stay with him."

Over the next three hours, as they tailed Batman from bar to bar in the Crime Alley district, Robin and Nightwing received a graphic lesson in what can happen when a hero takes the wrong path.

Batman left a trail of injured, bleeding hoodlums behind him, always the same question on his lips. "Where do I find LeHah?"

And eventually, after he'd all but wrecked a dockside tavern, he found someone who knew.

Batman stormed from the building, and Robin and Nightwing watched with a mixture of disbelief and horror as he threw back his head and raged at the night sky. "I'm coming for you, LeHah! The Angel of Vengeance knows where you are! Do you hear me, LeHah? You're going to die!"

As he leapt into the Batmobile and sped off, Nightwing spoke urgently to Robin. "This is getting out of hand! Try to get Bruce on the radio," he ordered. "I can't stand by and watch murder, not even an arms dealer like LeHah!"

Robin was tempted to argue; he wanted to go, too, to be where the action was. But he knew Nightwing was right. He unclipped his belt radio as his friend swung off toward the river.

The ugly, bald man known as LeHah and his surviving thugs were on the penthouse terrace of the riverside condo that his long trade in death had bought him. A hereditary member of the Order of

St. Dumas, he'd never paid any attention to the organization's eccentric ways until his father—the treasurer—died. He couldn't believe how much money the order had salted away, or the ease with which he was able to embezzle it.

When he'd been discovered, LeHah started to kill off the members one by one—only to be hunted down by their punishing angel, Azrael. But armor-piercing ammunition had ended the threat as he blew the so-called Angel of Vengeance away.

Now another creature of the night wished to foil his plans.

The billowing cape blotted out the moon as he swooped down on them. Gauntlets took the first two, a shuriken the third. The two survivors were downed by the high-intensity laser beam that flashed from his right knuckles. And all before even one of them could cry out.

LeHah raised his armor-piercing gun, only to drop it with a pained yell as Batman bathed it in flame from his right hand.

"You killed my father, LeHah," Jean Paul accused him. "You killed Azrael."

The bald man's mouth fell open. "You mean, you're—"

"I am the son of my father. As he was before me, I am Azrael, the Angel of Vengeance!"

On the last word Batman attacked, delivering a

rapid-fire series of blows. LeHah went down, blood on his white silk shirt.

Then out of nowhere whipped a bola, wrapping around Batman's hand.

Nightwing slammed into him, hurling them both against a potted palm, knocking it over.

"No more killing, Batman!" The teenager was atop him, his knee pinioning Batman's chest. "Let the law deal with him. This isn't the way!"

Batman hurled Nightwing off bodily. "I am Batman, Angel of Vengeance! No one gets in my way!"

*So Robin was right again,* Nightwing realized. *Paul's Batman role and his Azrael training are all mixed up—and the result is near-insanity!* Nightwing rolled, and a spiked fist thudded into the concrete where his head had been.

LeHah saw his chance as the two heroes fought and ran for the far end of the roof. His personal chopper sat waiting. He leapt inside, hit the ignition, and the rotors whirled into life. He could get out of this intact yet.

Nightwing put up his best show, but it wasn't enough. Paul was flying in crazy mode now, his mind a confused red blur, the System flooding him with energy as he unconsciously called on its vast resources. Finally Nightwing went down in a flurry of brutal blows. Nothing could stop Batman now . . .

Except, perhaps, one man.

"Enough!" a stern voice commanded. Batman turned . . .

. . . to find himself face-to-face with Batman!

But where Jean Paul Valley wore his high-tech creation of Kevlar, lightweight metal, and advanced weaponry, Bruce Wayne was dressed in the simple, classic bat-costume. The yellow oval, with its black bat silhouette, stood out proudly on his chest.

"One chance, Azrael. Lay your arms down now."

"Never! I am the true Batman!"

Both moved with blinding speed, feinting, parrying, striking . . . completely oblivious to the chopper that rose into the air at the far end of the roof. As LeHah circled, he saw the fighting men, and Robin nearby, kneeling beside the injured Nightwing. LeHah grinned savagely. *What an opportunity—!*

He sent the chopper diving down toward them, one hand on the controls, the semiautomatic in the other loosing a stream of armor-piercing lead out the window.

Robin and Nightwing were safe, protected by the angle of the raised plant beds, but the two Batmen were completely exposed. They rolled for safety as the heavy bullets spattered the balcony around them.

They were farther apart now, and Paul was first on his feet as the chopper started to wheel away.

Paul hesitated, torn two ways. On the one hand, there was Batman; on the other, he knew he couldn't let his father's killer escape.

As the chopper banked, he had one clear shot at LeHah. Too far for a shuriken to do much damage—but well within reach of his line. The grapnel shot out. He'd haul the murderer out of there!

But just as he fired, Bruce dived and took Paul around the waist. The grapnel was knocked off course, missing LeHah by yards—but clamping onto the craft's rear rotor.

The tough line wrapped around and around the rotor shaft, jerking Paul off his feet in a tug that carried them clear off the roof.

They swung to and fro like puppets, totally unable to control their wild gyrations as the crippled chopper swung crazily out of control. It was certain death to let go, and both men hung on grimly.

Suddenly the engine cut out; they hung for a timeless moment, then plunged down at ever-increasing speed.

Below them was the Gotham Narrows Bridge, its high suspension pillars rushing up to meet them.

At the last moment Bruce let go, extending his arm, tossing the line attached to his Batarang up and out. It caught on a thick suspension cable, jerking him away. Dimly he was aware of Paul flashing past him, dropping toward the dark waters below.

Then the world turned red and Bruce was almost blasted from his line as the chopper hit the pillar and exploded. LeHah didn't stand a chance.

Nightwing had recovered now, and he and Robin ran downstairs and out onto the street. The burning chopper hung like a metal skeleton from the crumbling pillar, the hot flames reflecting off the water. As they ran toward it, they saw the unmistakable figure of Paul, bobbing in the water, striking out hard for the other shore.

The Batmobile was parked where Paul had left it, a hundred yards away, and Bruce ran to it. It was locked, of course, and Paul had changed the electronic access codes. But Bruce had it open in less than a minute, sliding into the driver's seat even as Robin and Nightwing raced toward him. They were calling to him, but he had no time to stop and listen. He fired the engine—

"No!" Robin cried. "Paul made a lot of modifications! What if he's booby-trapped it?"

Robin pulled up in horror as the Batmobile erupted with a roar that sounded like the end of the world.

# Five

**S**omeone had called the emergency services, and sirens were wailing closer.

But Robin and Nightwing didn't hear, staring openmouthed at the inferno. *Bruce . . . he was in there! Nothing could have survived that blazing mess.*

"It's okay." Stunned, they could hardly believe Bruce's voice behind them. "As soon as I switched on the ignition I heard the difference in engine note," he explained. "So I hit the ejector seat."

Robin almost laughed out loud with relief. Then he remembered: "Paul! He got away!"

"There's only one place he could have gone. I know where to find him."

Nightwing rubbed his bruised arm, a little rueful. "I hate to tell you what to do," he began hesitantly, "but Paul's got a whole new bag of tricks. Maybe you should arm yourself."

Bruce stared ahead, out over the water. "I cannot stoop to his level to defeat him. If I'm unable to win unarmed, I don't deserve to win."

He had faced the man who beat the man who broke him . . . and not only was Bruce still alive, he was determined he would triumph. He knew he had Paul rattled.

Now he had to finish the job.

Once, when he was six years old, young Bruce had been playing on the grassy hillside that sloped away from the manor when he fell through a hole in the ground. A small opening at the bottom of the low chamber led into a narrow tunnel that gradually widened until it opened out into what would become the Batcave system.

It was this tunnel Bruce had used earlier to gain entrance to the Cave, and he used it again now, carefully replacing the turf sods that disguised its trapdoor. *Funny,* he thought, as he squeezed with difficulty between the tunnel's rock walls. *It seemed so much larger to a six-year-old.*

"I knew I'd find you here."
"*I* knew you'd find me here."

They stood in the vast Batcave, fifty yards apart, like old-time gunslingers readying for a showdown.

"One more time, Paul. Give it up. Hand over the mantle of the Bat."

But Bruce knew what the answer would be, and he was already tossing a Batarang as Paul's own arm came up to fire shurikens. The Batarang knocked one from the air, and the soft sigh from the launcher told him Paul's supply was exhausted. One danger removed.

He saw the laser glow, giving him just an instant to act before it flashed. He hurled himself back into the shadows, outside the pool of soft light, as the beam bore into the cave wall nearby.

"No use, Wayne," Paul laughed. "This Angel can see in the dark!"

Bruce had his own night visor in place. Nevertheless he ran, weaving and ducking up a meandering side tunnel. Laser beams hissed as they flared against the damp rock walls. It was wetter this far back in the underground cavern, and he remembered the small stream that gurgled across the tunnel.

Soft sandstone that had been eroded over the ages had gathered here to form a small beach. Bruce knelt to scoop up handfuls of the sand. As Paul rounded the corner and saw him, Bruce hurled the gritty mud. It splattered across Paul, a large lump sticking to his laser sights.

Another weapon negated!

But Paul was far from finished. A jet of flame flowed from his wrist. Bruce dived and rolled, splashing through the ice-cold shallow water, soaking himself as best he could for protection.

It was enough. The flame flickered and died, and he heard Paul curse. He didn't carry enough fuel to operate it at full intensity for long.

Now that Paul had no weapons left, it was Bruce who had a definite advantage. He knew these caves, knew every pothole and slippery rock, every stalagmite and stalactite, every dim and distant recess.

"Stop hiding behind that costume and mask," Bruce taunted him, backing away. "Take them off. Let me see who Jean Paul Valley really is!"

"I'm Batman!" Paul moved angrily after him, banging his shin painfully against a boulder, scraping his shoulder against the rough cave wall. He couldn't understand why the System wasn't kicking in. It had always helped him before when he was in trouble, always been there for him when he needed it most. It helped him beat the Tally Man, didn't it? And so many others—even Bane himself. *So why isn't it working now?* he wondered.

He didn't know the System had reached its limit. Every trick, every bit of fighting knowledge and daredevil ability that had been programmed into him was used up. The System didn't have any more to give. Jean Paul Valley was on his own now.

Again he stumbled into a curving wall and hurt his elbow as he backed into a stalagmite.

Even without weapons, Bruce knew Paul in his bulky armor would be a formidable foe. *There's been enough violence already,* he thought. *I need a way to take Paul out without hurting him—or myself!*

The answer came to Bruce in a flash. He backed away toward the hidden tunnel by which he'd entered, talking all the time. "You're a victim, Paul. Your father and his cursed order twisted your mind from infancy on! And you in turn abused the power I gave you. I trusted you with my city, Paul. You've let me down—and betrayed the people of Gotham!"

"Liar!" Paul lunged at him, missed, then followed as Bruce backed into the smaller entrance.

"That's why you need the costume and mask." Bruce kept his voice low. "They're armor, shields to hide the poor, scared victim inside you, while you strike back at the world that hurt you!"

"I told you—I'm Batman!" Paul almost screamed. "I'm Batman—or I'm nothing at all!"

The cave walls sloped in toward each other like a funnel, and the way became ever narrower and harder to negotiate. In his tight-fitting costume,

Bruce was barely able to continue his backward path. But Paul grunted as his bulky shoulder pads wedged firmly and brought him to a halt.

"You're a puppet, Paul." Bruce's voice was insistent. "But you don't *have* to be. You can be yourself!"

*"I am the Batman!"* Virtually shaking with rage, Paul wriggled free of the costume that was restraining him. Almost reduced to crawling on his belly now, he forced himself on, leaving his cape and body armor and gauntlets like the discarded skin of a serpent.

Where the tunnel ended, Bruce waited, listening to the drip of water, the flap of leathery bats' wings, and the grunts of the approaching man. *It's been a long night,* he was thinking, *but hopefully, it's almost over. It ought to be dawn now.* He reached up and slid the infrared sights from his mask.

Dressed in T-shirt and undershorts, his flesh scored by abrasions where the rough stone had scraped him, Paul hauled himself into the low chamber. Only his cowl was still in place.

"So," he said softly, "you've got no more room to run."

"Neither have you," Bruce replied. He reached up, grasping the catch that held the heavy trapdoor in place. "It's over, Paul. Please believe that."

Bruce tugged on the catch, the trapdoor swung

open—and bright sunlight flooded into the chamber. It washed over the startled Paul, stabbing into the night lenses that were meant only for darkness.

Paul screamed and tore off the mask, then collapsed, sobbing, to his knees. "I—I was wrong," he gasped, his voice suddenly young, almost childlike. "You are the Batman, Bruce. You've *always* been the Batman! While I . . . " The words caught in his throat, and he looked up through unseeing eyes. "I am nothing."

"You're wrong, Paul," Bruce told him. "You just don't know who you are—or what you might become." He took the younger man's arm and helped him shakily to his feet. "But you can learn."

Bruce scrambled up out of the hole into the bright daylight and reached back to haul Paul up behind him. *He looks so young,* Bruce thought. *So vulnerable.*

"It won't be easy," Bruce went on, "and you might fail. But you have to *try*. That's all any of us can do. Even heroes."

Blinking, his vision returning now, Paul turned to the man who had saved him. "Then you forgive me?"

Bruce thought for a moment. "Yes," he said at last. "I suppose I do. Someday, I may even forgive myself." He sighed. "Go now. And don't ever look back."

Paul took a faltering step, then another, and walked away down the grassy slope into the sunlight. Under the cowl, Bruce felt a bead of perspiration run down his face—relief, or the unaccustomed warmth of the sun? Day is no time for the Bat. He stood motionless, watching until Paul faded from view, before slipping back down into the cool welcoming depths of the cave.

A day later, and the neglected Wayne Manor was halfway back in shape. Tim took particular pleasure in tearing down Paul's brick walls with a hammer, while Alfred surveyed the damage, tutting and making a mental note of the likely cost.

"Whatever it costs," Bruce told him, "it'll be worth it. I have to say—it's good to be home!"

Commissioner Gordon looked out his window, and for the hundredth time thanked Mercy that the hideous neon billboard was still out of action.

A jagged-edged shadow crossed the moon, and he knew it was Batman. Only this time there was something different . . . the costume. The Darknight Detective looked the way he used to. In the old days. Four or five months ago. A lifetime in both their jobs.

Gordon leaned back in his chair and smiled to

himself. Sometimes—not very often, but some-times—he was glad he lived in Gotham City. He was glad he had this job. He was glad there was a Batman.

# Epilogue

**P**erched high on a ledge above the city, the Batman tastes the night air and scans the streets below with vigilant eyes.

He feels a kind of peace run through him. He belongs here. This is his city. The night is his friend.

He stiffens as he hears a cry, a muffled threat bourne up on the chill night breeze. Silently, he launches himself into the darkness.

When his city cries out, the Batman will always be there to answer.

# About the Author

**Alan Grant** was born in Bristol, England, in 1949 but spent his first twenty years near Edinburgh, Scotland, where his parents, daughter, both brothers, and their families still live. Leaving school when he was seventeen to pursue a career in accounting/banking, he quickly realized he had made a mistake and switched to publishing. He wanted to work in comics, his first love, but instead worked his way up to editor via a variety of romance publications, learning to write women's romantic fiction in the process and producing a successful run of teenage true confessions. He soon quit editorial work to go freelance and, after returning briefly to college, worked on the British comic book sensation *2000 AD*. For a while he became the Puzzle King of Fleet Street, specializing in cryptic crosswords and giant word search/quiz combos. Soon he started to write his first comic strips and went on to script *Judge Dredd*, among many other titles. He is also the coauthor of a series of children's prose anthologies and publisher of several creator-owned comic titles. Mr. Grant is currently the writer of *Batman: Shadow of the Bat* (a series created especially for him), *Lobo*, and many team-up and crossover titles, including the recently published *Batman/Spawn: War Devil*. Other titles he's written for DC include *Batman, Detective Comics, Batman/Judge Dredd, L.E.G.I.O.N.*, and *The Demon*. He has also written *The Incredible Hulk, The Punisher*, and *Robocop*, among other titles, for Marvel Comics. Alan Grant lives and works in a converted twelfth-century church near Colchester, England, with his wife and guardian angel Sue.

# About the Illustrators

**Graham Nolan** was born in 1962 in Englewood Cliffs, New Jersey, and grew up in Long Island and Florida. He studied at the Joe Kubert School of Cartoon and Graphic Art but broke into comics before graduating in 1985. Since then he has done freelance work in advertising, and for Marvel, Eclipse, and DC Comics. For DC, Graham has worked on a number of titles, including *Hawkworld, Metamorpho,* and *Vengeance of Bane.* He is currently drawing Batman in *Detective Comics,* the comic book where the Dark Knight made his debut in 1939. Mr. Nolan lives in East Aurora, New York, with his wife Julia, daughter Sarah, and basset hound Bijou (they also have a baby on the way).

**Scott Hanna** studied at Pratt Institute in Brooklyn, New York, and got his first solo work as a penciller and inker for Eternity Comics. A year later he started freelancing at DC Comics, where he is currently the inker of Batman in *Detective Comics*. He is also working on *Spider-Man* for Marvel Comics and has worked on *X-Force, Darkstars, Hawk & Dove, Robin,* and the highly acclaimed *Doom Patrol* series, among other titles. Scott Hanna is now happily married and lives in Bucks County, Pennsylvania, with his wife Pamela and their two cats.

**Joe DeVito** was born in 1957 in New York City and grew up in Berkeley Heights, New Jersey. A 1981 honors graduate of Parsons School of Design, he has painted hundreds of book covers, including several in Bantam's The Further Adventures paperback series, featuring Batman (Penguin and Catwoman), Superman, and Wonder Woman, as well as the Doc Savage series. He is a contributor to the upcoming visual novel *The Secret Oceans,* by Betty Ballantine. In addition, he has painted trading cards in the Star Wars Galaxy II and the DC Master Series, Lobo and Superman retail posters for DC Comics, and has sculpted a newly released Doc Savage statue for Graphitti Designs. Mr. DeVito currently lives in New Jersey with his wife Mary Ellen and daughter Melissa.